1

D1364296

The figure on the roof.

The man looked at me with something between horror and dismay. He raised a hand as if to prevent me from moving forward.

"No!" he shouted. "I d-d-didn't . . ."

Then he turned and ran.

I chased after him and that was when I discovered that I had miscalculated. I had run into the wrong store and there was a ten-foot gap between his roof and mine. But I hadn't come this far to let an impossible jump and a probable fall to my death seven floors below worry me. I picked up speed and threw myself off the edge.

ALSO BY ANTHONY HOROWITZ

The Greek Who Stole Christmas

A Diamond Brothers Mystery

ANTHONY HOROWITZ

PUFFIN BOOKS

PUFFIN BOOKS

Published by the Penguin Group

Penguin Young Readers Group, 345 Hudson Street, New York, New York 10014, U.S.A.

Penguin Group (Canada), 90 Eglinton Avenue East, Suite 700, Toronto, Ontario, Canada M4P 2Y3
(a division of Pearson Penguin Canada Inc.)

Penguin Books Ltd, 80 Strand, London WC2R 0RL, England

Penguin Ireland, 25 St Stephen's Green, Dublin 2, Ireland (a division of Penguin Books Ltd)

Penguin Group (Australia), 250 Camberwell Road, Camberwell, Victoria 3124, Australia
(a division of Pearson Australia Group Pty Ltd)

Penguin Books India Pvt Ltd, 11 Community Centre, Panchsheel Park, New Delhi - 110 017, India

Penguin Group (NZ), 67 Apollo Drive, Rosedale, North Shore 0632, New Zealand
(a division of Pearson New Zealand Ltd)

Penguin Books (South Africa) (Pty) Ltd, 24 Sturdee Avenue,
Rosebank, Johannesburg 2196, South Africa

Registered Offices: Penguin Books Ltd, 80 Strand, London WC2R 0RL, England

First published in Great Britain by Walker Books Ltd, 2007
First published in the United States of America by Puffin Books,
a division of Penguin Young Readers Group, 2008

Copyright © Stormbreaker Productions Ltd, 2007

LIBRARY OF CONGRESS DATA IS AVAILABLE

Puffin Books ISBN 978-0-14-240375-4

Printed in the United States of America

CONTENTS

The Greek Who Stole Christmas

DEATH THREAT

I knew it was going to be a bad Christmas when I walked past the charity shop and the manager ran out and tried to offer me charity. It seemed that everyone in Camden Town knew I was broke. Even the turkeys were laughing at me. On the last day of term, the teachers passed the hat around for me . . . not that I really needed a hat, but I suppose it's the thought that counts. Christmas was just a few weeks away and the only money I had was a ten-buck gift certificate that my parents had sent me from Australia. I tried to swap it for hard cash at my local bookstore, but the manager—a thin-faced woman in her forties—was completely heartless.

"I need to eat," I explained.

"Then buy a cookbook."

"I can't afford the ingredients!"

"I'm sorry. You can only use a gift certificate to buy books."

"What's the point of buying books if I'm too faint to read?"

She smiled sadly at me. "Have you tried Philip Pullman?"

"No. Do you think he'd lend me some money?"

I couldn't believe my parents had sent me a gift certificate for Christmas, but then, of course, they had no idea about anything. My dad had moved them to Sydney a few years before—he was a door-to-door salesman, selling doors, and he must have been doing well because this year he'd printed his own Christmas card. HAVE AN A-DOOR-ABLE CHRISTMAS, it said on the cover. There was a picture of a kangaroo with a red hat on, looking out of an open door. I was still laughing as I ripped it to pieces. My parents had two new kids now: Doreen and Dora. Two sisters I'd never met. That made me sad sometimes. They weren't even two years old and they probably had more spare cash than me.

I was thinking about Australia as I walked home from the bookstore. My mum and dad had wanted to take me with them when they emigrated, and maybe it had been a mistake to slip off the plane before it took off. While it was taxiing down the runway, I was running away to find a taxi—and they hadn't even noticed until they were thirty-five thousand feet above France. Apparently my mum had hysterics. And my dad had my lunch.

I'm still not sure it was a smart decision. They say that London is like a village, and I certainly enjoyed living there. The only trouble was, I'd moved in with the village idiot. I'm talking, of course, about my big brother, Herbert Timothy Simple. But that wasn't what he called himself. He called himself Tim Diamond, Private Detective—and that's what it said in the Yellow Pages, along with the line:

"No problem too problematic." He'd written that himself.

Tim was the worst private detective in England. I mean . . . he'd just spent two weeks working in a big department store in the West End. He was supposed to be looking out for shoplifters, but I don't think he'd kept his eye on the ball. In fact, the ball was the first thing that got stolen. After that, things went from bad to worse. The store had twenty-three departments when he started but only sixteen when he left. He was fired, of course. The dummies in the window probably had a higher IQ than Tim. He was lucky he had me. I solved the crimes, Tim got the credit. That was how it worked. If you've read my other stories, you'll know what I'm talking about. If you haven't, go out and buy the books. If you like, I'll even sell you a ten-buck gift certificate. You can have it for nine bucks.

Anyway, right now Tim was out of work. And November had arrived like a bad dog, snapping at everyone in the street and sending them hurrying home. As usual, it wasn't going to snow—but the pipes were frozen, the pud-dles had iced over, and you could see people's breath in the air.

They were playing a Christmas carol on the radio as I let myself in. Tim was sitting at his desk wrapped in a blanket, trying to open a can of sardines that was so far past its sell-by date he'd probably have more luck selling it as an antique.

I threw myself into a chair. "Any news?" I asked. "I don't suppose anyone has offered you a job?"

"I just don't get it," Tim replied. "You'd think someone, somewhere, would need a pri-vate detective. Why is no one hiring me?"

"Maybe it's because you're no good," I said.

"You might be right." Tim nodded sadly.

"There are police dogs that have solved more crimes than you."

"Yes," Tim agreed, "but at least I don't have fleas."

I got up and turned the radio off. Tim had managed to get the can open and the room was suddenly filled with the smell of twenty-seven-year-old sardines. And it was just then that there was a knock on the door.

I looked at Tim. Tim looked at me. We had a client and we also had a room that looked like a garbage dump and smelled like the River Thames during the Great Plague.

"One minute!" Tim shouted.

In that one minute, we raced around like two people in a speeded-up commercial for dish soap. Papers went into drawers. Plates went into the kitchen. The sardines went into the trash can and the trash can went out the window. Sixty seconds later, the office looked more like an office and Tim was sitting behind his desk with a straightened tie and a crooked smile. I took one last look around and opened the door.

A man walked in. I guessed he was in his forties: short and fat, smoking a cigar. The cigar was short and fat too. He was dressed in a nasty suit. The pattern was so loud you could almost hear it coming. He had black, greasy hair, thick lips, and eyes that would have been nicer if they'd matched. His shoes had been polished until you could see your face in them—though with his face, I wouldn't have bothered. There was a gold signet ring on his finger. The way it squeezed the flesh, I doubted it would ever come off.

"You always keep your clients waiting outside?" he demanded as he came in and took a chair.

"We were filing," Tim explained.

He looked around. "I don't see no filing cabinets." He spoke like an American but he wasn't one. He was just someone who spent too much time on planes.

"We were filing our nails," I said.

He helped himself to one of Tim's business cards from the desk. "Are you Tim Diamond?"

"Yeah. That's me." Tim narrowed his eyes. He always does that when he's trying to look serious. Unfortunately it just makes him look nearsighted. "I'm a private eye."

"I know," the man growled. "That's why I'm here. My name is Jake Hammill and I want to hire you."

"You want to hire me?" Tim couldn't believe it. He leaned forward. "So what can I do for you, Mr. Camel?"

"Not Camel. I'm Jake Hammill. You want me to spell it for you?"

"N-O," Tim said.

"I work in the music industry. As a matter of fact, I'm the manager of a woman who's a very famous pop singer."

Tim scowled. "If she's so famous, how come I've never heard of her?"

"I haven't told you her name yet."

"Maybe it would help if you did."

Hammill glanced at me. He was obviously suspicious. He turned back to Tim. "Can you keep a secret?" he asked.

"I'm not going to tell you," Tim replied.

"All right." Hammill nodded. "Her name is Minerva."

I have to admit, I was surprised. Hammill looked pretty small-time to me, but Minerva was one of the biggest names in the business. She was a multimillionaire pop singer and a movie actress. I doubted there was anyone in the world who hadn't seen her videos. She was the woman with the golden voice and the silver-plated breasts. Her clothes were outrageous—like the rest of her lifestyle. She had been born in Greece, but now she lived most of the time in New York. The fact that she was visiting London had made the front page of every newspaper . . . even the *Financial Times*.

"The thing is," Hammill said, "I've got a serious problem . . ." He twisted his signet ring nervously around his finger like he was trying to take it off. "Listen to me," he went on. "Minerva has been invited over here for Christmas. Tomorrow she's turning on the Christmas lights in Regent Street. And on Thursday at midday she's opening the Santa Claus workshop at Harrods department store in Knightsbridge. There's going to be a lot of press. A lot of TV. It's great publicity. But this is the problem . . ." He drew a breath. "I think she's in danger."

"What makes you think that?" I asked.

"Well, yesterday she received an anonymous letter."

"An anonymous letter!" Tim exclaimed. "Who from?"

Hammill scowled. "I don't know. It was anonymous. But it threatens her with death."

"So where is this letter, Mr. Hubble?" Tim asked.

"It was sent to Minerva. She's got it. I'd like you to come and meet her at her hotel and she'll take you through it."

"She'll take me through the hotel?"

"No. She'll take you through the letter." He leaned forward and already I could see the doubt in his face. "I have to say, Mr. Diamond, I need to be sure you're the right man for this job. I wanted to go to the police, but Minerva's husband insisted that a private detective would be better. I understand you advertise in the Yellow Pages."

"Yeah," I muttered. "They match his teeth."

"I take it you know how to look after yourself," Hammill said.

Tim looked puzzled. "But I'm not ill!" he muttered.

Hammill rolled his eyes. Maybe I was

imagining things, but I could have sworn they went in opposite directions. "I'm not asking about your health," he said. "I need someone to stay close to Minerva while she's in London, and that may mean getting into a fight. So what I'm asking you is—do you know judo or karate?"

"Sure!" Tim nodded. "Judo, karate, and origami. When do you want me to start, Mr. Rubble?"

It was obvious to me that Hammill was having second thoughts about Tim. And maybe third and fourth thoughts too. For a moment he bit his fingernail, deep in thought. Maybe he had plans to bite all the way down to the signet ring. Then he came to a decision. "All right," he said. "Minerva is staying at the Porchester Hotel, which is in Hyde Park. That's highly confidential information, by the way."

"What do you mean?" Tim demanded. "Everyone knows that the Porchester Hotel is in Hyde Park."

"Sure. But nobody knows she's staying

there. Otherwise we'd have fans all over the place."

"That would help with the ventilation . . ."

"Minerva likes her privacy. She's booked in under the name of Mrs. Smith. Room sixteen. I want you to visit her this evening. Say, seven o'clock?"

"Seven o'clock," Tim said obediently.

"That's right. I'll let her take a look at you, and if she thinks you're up to it, you're hired."

Tim nodded. I knew what was coming next. He was sitting back in his chair with his feet resting on his desk, trying to look every inch the private detective. The fact that he had a hole in one of his shoes didn't help. As far as he was concerned, he was back in business. And he was determined to prove it. "What about my fee?" he demanded.

"You're not hired yet," Hammill reminded him.

"Okay, Mr. Rabble. But I'd better let you know now, I'm not cheap. The only thing that goes cheap in this office is my parakeet, and I don't think your superstar wants a bodyguard with feathers."

Hammill tried to make sense of this, decided it wasn't worth trying, and stood up. "I'll see you this evening," he said. One last twist of the ring. It wasn't going anywhere, but he was. He walked out of the office, slamming the door behind him.

There was a moment's silence.

I went over to the cupboard and searched through the CDs. I knew we'd have a Minerva recording somewhere and, sure enough, there it was—her third album, *Think Pink*. I looked at the face on the cover: the blond hair, the green eyes, the lips that looked like they could suck in a horse. Not for the first time I wished we had a CD player, but Tim had pawned it months ago. Along with just about everything else. That was another sad thought. When I walked into the Camden Town pawnshop, I felt more at home than I did at home.

But maybe our luck was going to change. All Tim had to do was protect her for a couple of days and there'd be a handsome check at the end of it. He might even end up taking a bullet for her. If so, I just hoped they'd pay him extra. And whatever happened, it might be fun to hang out with one of the biggest entertainers on the planet.

"I can't believe it!" I said. "We're going to meet Minerva!"

"It's even better than that," Tim replied. "She's opening Santa's workshop at Harrods. Maybe we'll meet Father Christmas!"

I slid the CD back into the cupboard.

Minerva had just received a death threat and her husband had hired Tim Diamond. That was like getting her a knitted cardigan when what she really needed was a bulletproof vest. Well, one thing was certain: this was going to be a Christmas to remember. I just wondered if Minerva would still be around to see in the New Year.

SUITE SIXTEEN

The Porchester was in the middle of London's Park Lane, a five-star hotel that cost the earth. The sort of place I wouldn't be able to stay in a blue moon. You could tell it was expensive: I spotted two celebrities in the revolving doors, and by the time I'd reached the reception desk, I'd passed three more. There was enough fur and jewelry in that place to fill a store. And that was just the men.

The reception area was all glass and marble, including the receptionist's dress. That's fashion for you. Tim and I had arrived half an hour early to drink in the atmosphere—and looking at the prices in the hotel bar, we certainly weren't going to be drinking anything else. A glass of water here cost the same as a glass of wine anywhere else, and for a glass of wine you needed to take out a loan. Nothing cost peanuts here . . . not even the peanuts. That's the thing about the super rich. They don't mind when things are crazily expensive. It just reminds them how rich they are.

We went over to the reception desk and asked to see "Mrs. Smith." The receptionist was a slinky-looking girl with long fingernails. She had perfect teeth, but she didn't smile and she spoke through her nose, so I guessed she didn't like showing them. She picked up a telephone and dialed a number with a fingernail that was a little longer than her finger. She spoke for a few seconds, then put the phone down. Her earrings jangled. So did my nerves.

"The second floor," she said, barely moving her lips. Maybe she was training to be a ventriloquist. "It's suite sixteen."

So Minerva had a suite, not a single room. We took the elevator to the second floor and I have to admit I enjoyed the journey. It's the only elevator I've ever seen with solid gold buttons and a chandelier. I could see Tim staring at everything as if he'd just died and gone to heaven. He'd insisted on putting on a suit, which he'd found at the bottom of the closet. It was just a shame that the moths had found it first. Still, so long as nobody wondered why the jacket had seventeen buttonholes but only seven buttons, he'd be fine.

The elevator door opened and we found ourselves in a corridor with about a mile of pink carpet, more chandeliers, and the sort of wallpaper that seemed wasted on a wall. Suite sixteen was about halfway down—a double wooden door with gold numbers on it.

Tim raised his hand, about to knock. And that was when we heard it. A sudden loud crack from the other side. A gunshot? I wasn't so sure, but Tim had no doubt at all. His eyes widened and he threw himself at the door—shoulder first—obviously intending to smash it down, climb through the wreckage, and rescue Minerva from whoever was taking potshots at her. It didn't budge. Tim howled as he dislocated his shoulder. I reached out and opened the door. It was unlocked anyway.

We ran in. The door led straight into a plush living room. There were three people there. One of them was Jake Hammill, the manager who had come to our office that afternoon. The other was an older man dressed in a velvet jacket with a silk cravat around his neck. He had one of those permanent suntans that give your skin the color of a peach but the texture of a prune. The third was Minerva. I recognized her at once with that strange buzz of excitement you get when you find yourself face-to-face with someone really famous. She was holding half a Christmas cracker. The tanned man was holding the other half. Well, that explained the bang we had just heard.

"Who the hell are you?" the older man asked.

"I'm Tim Diamond." Tim shrugged and I heard a loud click as his shoulder blade somehow managed to slip back into place. Well, that was something. Minerva looked as if she was about to call the police. At least she wouldn't have to ask for an ambulance too.

"So what do you mean just bursting in here?" the man continued. "Haven't you ever heard of knocking?"

"Wait a minute! Wait a minute!" Hammill interjected. "This is the private detective I was telling you about. The one you told me to see. Tim Diamond."

"What about the kid?" the man asked.

"I'm his little brother, Nick," I said.

"Yeah, well . . . you'd better sit down."

Minerva had been watching all this with a mixture of puzzlement and disbelief. I sat down on the sofa next to her, thinking that a million kids would have given their right arm to be where I was right now and wondering what she'd do with a million right arms. She was dressed simply in expensive jeans and a white shirt, but even so she was one of the most beautiful women I'd ever seen. She had long blond hair, eyes that were somewhere between blue and green, and the sort of body that made me wish I was older than fourteen.

Maybe she was smaller than I'd imagined, but then I don't have much imagination. And looking at her, I didn't need it. She was the real thing and she was right there next to me.

Meanwhile, Tim had sat down in a chair. I could tell he fancied Minerva too. As far as I know, Tim has never had a steady girlfriend. He just simply hasn't had any luck finding a woman who's attracted to a twenty-eight-year-old with no money and no brains. To be fair to Tim, he's not that unattractive. I mean, he's slim and he's dark and he's reasonably fit. And it seemed to me that Minerva was definitely interested in him. Mind you, if the old, wrinkled guy was her husband, I wasn't that surprised. How did a world-famous sex symbol end up married to her grandfather?

"So—how can I help you?" Tim asked with a lazy smile. He crossed one leg over the other and his foot caught a lamp, sending the shade flying.

"I told you," Hammill growled. "Minerva needs a bodyguard."

"With a body like that I'm not surprised!" Tim agreed.

"Hold on!" the old man interrupted. "That's my wife you're talking about."

"And who are you?" Tim asked.

"I'm her husband!" He was perched on the arm of the sofa next to Minerva. "My name is Harold Chase." He laid a hand on Minerva's shoulder, and maybe I was wrong, but I could have sworn she shuddered slightly. "I'm paying you to make sure nobody hurts my baby."

"You've got a baby?" Tim demanded.

"I'm talking about Minerva!"

"I don't need looking after," Minerva said. They were the first words she had spoken, and I could hear the faint Greek accent fighting to get out. I was also reminded that this was the voice that had sold a billion CDs. "I don't need looking after;" it almost sounded like the title of one of her songs.

"We've got to take control of this situation," Hammill cut in. "You read what that letter said. Show it to Mr. Diamond."

Minerva thought for a moment, then pulled a white envelope out of her pocket. She held it for a moment. "This arrived yesterday," she said. "It was slipped under the door of my suite. It's from somebody who hates me."

Tim opened the letter and read aloud:

"Dear Minerva,

You are a monster. I cannot foregive you for what you did in Tropojë last summer. How could you do that? I will never forget it and very soon I am going to kill you. Your life will come to an end in London. This will be your last Christmas!"

Tim lowered the letter. "What makes you think that whoever wrote this hates you?" he asked.

Minerva stared at him. "I'm sorry?" she quavered.

"Well, he does call you *dear* Minerva . . ."

I snatched up the letter. It was straight out of a computer: blue ink on a plain sheet of paper. I noticed that whoever had written it couldn't spell *forgive*. The envelope was addressed: *Minerva, Suite 16.*

"What happened in Tropojë?" I asked.

"Nothing happened in Tropojë," Harold replied.

"It's the concert," Hammill cut in. "It's gotta be!"

"Forget it, Jake."

"No, Harry. They might as well know." Hammill turned to us. "It was just one of those things," he explained. "It happened last summer, like the letter says. Minerva was going to give a big charity concert in Albania. It was to benefit OAK."

"What's OAK?"

"Overweight Albanian Kids. It tries to help kids who watch too much TV and eat too much McDonald's. Some of them have to wear elasticized clothing. Many of them are in wheelchairs. They can walk—they're just too lazy. Anyway, they were really looking forward to the concert, but at the last moment Minerva had to pull out."

"Why?" I asked.

"I had a headache," Minerva replied. Obviously the overweight kids of OAK had never given her much cause for concern. Until now.

"You upset a lot of fans, Minerva," Jake said.

"And you think one of the fans is out to get her?"

"That's what it looks like."

I wasn't so sure. The idea of an oversize Albanian TV addict traveling all the way to England to kill Minerva sounded a bit far-fetched to me. On the other hand, there was that spelling mistake: English clearly wasn't the culprit's first language. But there was something about the letter I didn't like—and I don't just mean the death threat. I knew there was something wrong. Something didn't add up. But I hadn't yet had time to work out what it was.

"My own feeling is that we should just get out of London," the husband said. "I can't sleep with the thought of you being in danger."

"Harold—you're exaggerating!" Minerva shook her head. "This trip is great publicity. Turning on the lights and opening the work-shop is a big deal. I'm not going to run away just because some freak writes me a stupid letter." She turned to Tim. "I've got a single coming out on December twenty-fifth," she said.

"What's it called?" I asked.

Tim sighed. "It's called Christmas Day, Nick," he said. "Everyone knows that."

"I mean—what's the single called?"

"It's a song about cowboys," Minerva said. "The title is 'Like a Virginian.'" She fell silent for a moment and then she really surprised me. "If you boys are going to work with me, you might as well know that I hate this damn country and I hate Christmas."

"Minerva—" Harold began.

"Shut up, Harold! I just want to put my cards on the table."

"Your Christmas cards?" Tim asked.

"I don't have any. Those stupid pictures of angels and three wise men. If they were so wise, what was all that business with the gold, frankincense, and myrrh? You think a baby's got any use for that sort of stuff?" She shook her head. "I hate everything about Christmas. Those stupid Christmas trees that drop needles all over the carpet. Those boring carols that go on and on. Santa Claus with his stupid beard."

"What about Christmas presents?" I asked.

"Why would I care about Christmas presents? I've got everything I want already." She realized she was still holding the half cracker that she had pulled with her husband when we came in. "And I don't like these stupid crackers either," she went on. "They were sent up to the room by some fan or someone and all they've given me is a headache. As far as I'm concerned, the best thing to do with Christmas would be to forget the whole thing."

She threw down the cracker. A silver acorn and a slip of paper rolled out onto the table.

I don't know what it was that made me pick up the piece of paper. Maybe after Minerva's little speech I needed a laugh. Or maybe there was something about it that whispered to me that actually it didn't belong in a cracker. Anyway, I unfolded it, and sure enough there was the same blue ink as the letter, the same typeface. There were just two lines.

When Minerva sees the lights
that's when I'll have her in my sights

I read it out loud.

"I don't get it," Tim said. "It's not very funny . . ."

"It's not a joke, Tim!" I exclaimed. "It's another death threat."

"But that's impossible!" Harold seized the piece of paper and held it with a shaking hand. "How did this get inside the cracker?" he demanded. He stared at Jake Hammill. "You brought them up here!" he continued accusingly. "What's going on?"

"I just picked them up from reception!" Hammill replied. "They said they'd been left in your name by a fan."

"What does it mean?" Minerva asked. Her voice had gone quiet.

Nobody spoke—so I did. "It must mean tomorrow," I said. "When you turn on the Christmas lights." I picked up the acorn. It was heavy—solid silver, maybe. "And look at this," I said.

"An acorn . . ." Tim was puzzled.

"Off an *oak* tree, Tim," I said. "They're telling you who it came from."

"Of course!" Harold Chase stood up. He was shaking so much, I was worried something was going to fall off. "That's it," he said. "We're not going to turn on the lights. Forget it. We're not going anywhere near them."

"Harold . . ." Hammill began.

"I mean it, Jake."

"Forget it, Harold!" Minerva had also gotten to her feet. "Look—I've already promised. I'm going to turn on these stupid lights. I've got to be there: the mayor of London is coming. All the media will be out. It's going to be a big event."

"It'll be an even bigger event if someone shoots you," I muttered.

Tim turned to me. "That's a terrible thing to say, Nick!" He thought for a moment. "Anyway, they might not shoot her. They might run her over or blow her up or possibly fix the wires so she gets electrocuted . . ."

Minerva had gone a little pale. "Do you think you can protect me, Mr. Diamond?" she asked.

Tim smiled. "I'm the private eye who never blinks," he replied. "And from this moment I'm not going to let you out of my sight. I'm going to walk with you, eat with you, and go to bed with you—"

"Hey! Wait a minute! I'm in the bed!" Harold interrupted.

"We have a four-poster," Minerva said.

"That's great," Tim said. "We can have one post each."

Jake Hammill stepped forward. "I think Minerva will be safe enough while she's here at the Porchester Hotel," he said. "Suppose Mr. Diamond joins us tomorrow evening on the way to Regent Street?"

Minerva nodded. "I'm staying in all day tomorrow. That'll be fine."

"That just leaves the question of your fee, Mr. Diamond," Hammill continued.

"No question about it," Tim said. "I want one."

"Of course." Hammill blinked uncertainly. "We'll pay you two hundred a day. But let's get one thing straight. If anyone takes a shot at Minerva, we'll expect you to step in front of the bullet."

"Don't worry!" Tim jerked a thumb at me. "That's what he's for."

So there it was, signed and sealed. I still wondered why Minerva hadn't gone straight to the police—but maybe it wouldn't suit her being surrounded by the men in blue. I wanted to tell her that Tim would offer her about as much protection as a paper umbrella in the rain, but two hundred dollars was two hundred dollars. I watched as Jake Hammill counted out the money, and it occurred to me that I hadn't expected to see that many presidents without visiting Mount Rushmore. But here were twenty little portraits sliding into Tim's outstretched hand. I almost wanted to kiss them. Or him.

We took the bus home. We could have afforded a cab, but we'd already decided to blow a big chunk of the money on a three-course meal at our local Italian place. I was already dreaming of a twelve-inch pizza on an eleven-inch plate. Extra cheese and pepperoni. And maybe extra pizza too. But even so, I couldn't get Minerva out of my mind. I went over what had happened in the suite. I was still certain something was wrong.

"If you ask me, Tim, there's something strange about this," I said.

Tim looked around him. "It's just a bus, Nick," he said.

"I'm not talking about the bus. I'm talking about Minerva. Those death threats! Whoever heard of a death threat inside a Christmas cracker?"

"Yeah." Tim nodded. "And there was no sign of a paper hat."

I shook my head. "I wouldn't be surprised if they weren't making the whole thing up . . . the three of them. You heard what she said. All she wants to do is sell her CDs. Maybe the whole thing's just a publicity stunt."

Tim shook his head. "I don't think so, Nick. I think she's in real danger. Don't ask me why—I've just got an instinct for this sort of thing. A sixth sense."

"Sure," I muttered. "It's just a shame you missed out on the other five."

I looked out of the window. It had gotten

dark a while ago and it looked as if it was going to snow. There were a few flakes dancing in the wind. As we turned a corner, I noticed a man standing on the pavement with a sandwich board. He was handing out leaflets about the end of the world. London is full of people like that. Maybe it's the city that drives them mad or maybe they're mad before they arrive and it's the city that attracts them. Anyway, this man had three words in red paint across his chest:

DEATH WILL COME

He seemed to catch my eye as we went past. And I found myself wondering. Was he just a harmless crank trying to sell religion to anyone who would listen?

Or did he know something I didn't?

REGENT STREET

Everyone makes a fuss about the Christmas lights on Regent Street and maybe there was a time when they were actually worth traveling in to see. I remember when I was small, my mom would take me into town and the lights would flicker and flash and sparkle and people would cross the road with their necks craned, staring at them in wonderment, and they wouldn't even complain when they were run over by the 139 bus.

But that was then. Nowadays the lights are more or less the same as they are on any other main street at Christmas. Worse than that, they're paid for by big business, so you don't just get Santa, stars, or whatever. You get the latest characters from a Disney movie. Or "Harry Christmas" from J. K. Rowling. Or whatever.

Even so, turning on the lights is still a big deal. If it isn't a member of the royal family, it's a pop star or a Hollywood actor. All the newspapers and TV stations record the moment when the button gets pressed, and the next day you can read all about it on page one: MINERVA LIGHTS UP LONDON. And just for one day the earthquakes and the wars and the dirty politics are left to page two.

We were driven to Regent Street in a stretch limo. The chauffeur was a tall, slim man in a gray uniform and I couldn't help wondering if someone hadn't stretched him too. Minerva and her husband sat in the backseat. For the first time I noticed he was wearing a hearing aid, but he didn't need it because no one was talking to him. She was gazing out of the window. It was made from special glass so that no one could look in. Her manager, Jake Hammill, had the next seat to himself. Tim and I were closest to the front—and farthest from the bar. The three of them were drinking champagne, but all we'd been offered was a glass of ice water. Well, we were staff. Official security and its younger brother.

As usual Minerva was in a bad mood, but I had to admit that from where I was sitting she looked fabulous. She was wearing a bright red number with white fur trim. Think Santa Claus only thirty years younger and after major cosmetic surgery. Her lips were bright red too, shaped like a perfect kiss. It would have been hard to believe that this was the woman who hated Christmas. She'd done herself up like the sort of present every man in London would want to open. I glanced at Tim and saw that he was drooling. I just hoped it wouldn't stain the carpet.

"Now remember!" Harold Chase said to his wife. She turned around slowly and looked at him without a lot of interest. "You pose for the cameras. You make a little speech. You turn on the lights. And then we get the hell out of there."

"What's the big worry?" Minerva drawled.

"The big worry?" Harold's eyes bulged. For a nasty minute I thought they were going to fall out of his face. "There could be a killer out there, baby. You're going to be out in the open, exposed. Anyone could take a shot at you." He leaned forward and turned to Tim. "You'd better keep your eyes open, Mr. Diamond," he said.

"You don't have to worry, Mr. Cheese," Tim assured him. "I've had my eyes on your wife all evening."

"Well, you'd just better make sure nothing goes wrong."

"What could possibly go wrong with me around?" Tim exclaimed. He threw his hands back in a gesture of surprise, emptying his glass of ice water over the driver.

The car drew to a halt. It was just before six o'clock on a cold, dry Tuesday evening, but the stores were still open and there were Christmas shoppers everywhere. We got out and suddenly the night seemed to explode in a thousand flashes. They came so thick and fast that I found myself blinded. It was as if I had entered an electrical storm that signaled the end of the world.

Of course it was nothing so dramatic. Minerva was being photographed by a huge pack of press photographers, all of them holding up great, chunky cameras with lenses that were definitely pleased to see her. For a few seconds Minerva seemed to be frozen, half in the car and half out of it. Then she came to her senses and began to smile and wave; the silent, bad-tempered woman who had been sitting opposite me was instantly replaced by the perfect star that she was as the lights flashed all around her. And at that moment I got an idea of what it must be like to be a celebrity—loved not because of what you are but because of what the cameras want you to be.

At the same time I was puzzled. Minerva had received two death threats. Even if she had decided not to take them seriously, her husband and manager had been worried enough to hire Tim and me. And yet here she was completely surrounded by photographers. It occurred to me that any one of them could have a gun. There were a few policemen around, but right now killing Minerva would be the easiest thing in the world. I said nothing. I could only stand there as she turned and smiled and smiled and turned while the photographers shouted at her from every side.

"Over here, Minerva!"

"Give us a smile, Minerva!"

"This way, Minerva!"

Tim nudged me. He was standing with his back to the car, blinking in the camera flashes, but I could see that he was suddenly alert. I followed his eyes and saw a rather shabby-looking man in a suit hurrying toward us and suddenly I knew what was going to happen.

"Leave this to me . . ." Tim muttered.

"No, Tim!" I began.

But it was too late. Tim charged forward and grabbed hold of the man, then spun him around and threw him onto the hood of the limousine.

"That's far enough!" Tim exclaimed.

"I . . . I . . . I . . ." The man was too shocked to speak.

"What do you want with Minerva?" Tim demanded.

"I'm the mayor of London!" the man exclaimed.

Tim looked suspicious. He was still pinning him down. "The mayor of London is supposed to wear a red cloak and a pointy hat. If you're the mayor, where's the hat and cloak, eh?"

"I'm not that sort of mayor," the man growled. "I think you've been watching too many children's plays."

"Oh no I haven't!" Tim replied.

By now, two policemen had appeared and had pulled Tim away, helping the mayor to his feet. Because it *was* the mayor, of course. I'd recognized him instantly—his bald head, his brightly colored cheeks, and his entirely colorless mustache. Jake Hammill had seen what had happened. He hurried over and placed himself between the mayor and Tim.

"I'm so sorry!" he said. "We've hired private security and I guess he was a little jumpy."

"It's an outrage," the mayor exclaimed. He had a whiny voice.

"Come and meet Minerva, Mr. Mayor. She's been longing to say hello."

The thought of shaking Minerva's hand—or indeed any part of her—must have cheered the mayor up because he seemed to have forgotten that he had just been attacked by Tim. Hammill took him over to his client, who was still posing for the cameras. "Minerva . . . this is the mayor!" he said.

"How lovely to meet you, Mr. Mayor!" Minerva sounded so genuine, I almost believed her myself. She kissed him on the cheek and night became day again as the photographers captured the moment for the morning's headlines. "Where do we go to turn on the lights?" she asked.

"This way . . ." The mayor had gone red.

We made our way to a raised platform that had been constructed at the side of the street. There must have been four or five hundred people all around us, many of them waving autograph books and flashing cameras of their own. A Salvation Army band was playing carols. They finished "Away in a Manger" and began a version of "Silent Night" that was anything but.

Minerva climbed the stairs and I couldn't stop myself thinking of gallows and public hangings. I remembered the warning inside the cracker. Was someone really about to have a crack at her? I tried to think where I would hide myself if I were a sniper. I looked up at the rooftops. It was hard to see anything in the darkness, but there didn't seem to be anyone there. How about an open window? All the windows in the street were closed. Then maybe in the crowd . . .

By now Minerva had reached the top of the stairs. Was she being brave or stupid? Or was it just that she refused to take any of this seriously?

Jake Hammill was certainly looking nervous. So was Harold Chase. He was standing to one side, his hands in his pockets, pulling his black cashmere coat around him like he was trying to hide in it. His eyes were darting left and right. Even if nobody took a shot at his wife, I'd have said a major heart attack was a strong possibility. He didn't look like he'd last the night.

So there we all were on the platform: Minerva and the mayor at the front, the rest of us grouped behind. There was a single red button, mounted on a wooden block, and a microphone. Minerva stepped forward. The crowd fell silent. The Salvation Army players came to the end of a verse and stopped—unfortunately not all at the same time.

"Ladies and gentlemen!" It was the mayor speaking. His voice whined the full length of Regent Street and it wasn't just the fault of the microphone. "I'd like to welcome you all here. We've had some great stars turn on the lights in Regent Street. But this year, if you ask me, we've got the biggest star of all. Please welcome . . . Minerva!"

Everyone clapped and cheered.

"Thank you. Thank you so very much!" Minerva's voice echoed after the mayor's. "I'm so thrilled to be here, at Christmas. It's such a wonderful time of the year—the birth of baby Jesus and of course my new CD is about to be released. So Happy Christmas to everyone, and here goes . . ."

She lifted her finger.

And that was when it happened.

There were two gunshots. They sounded incredibly close and there could be no doubt that Minerva was the target. At once the entire atmosphere changed. There was a single second of frozen silence and then screams as the crowd panicked and began to scatter, people pushing one another to get out of the way. The band was swept away in the stampede. I saw someone fall into the big drum. The cymbal player was knocked off her feet with a final crash. On the platform, the mayor had been the first to dive for cover. Minerva hadn't moved, as if unsure what to do. I couldn't see if she had been hit or not. With that bright red dress, it was hard to tell.

Then Tim leaped into action. I have to hand it to him—at least he was braver than the mayor, who had curled into a ball in the corner of the platform with his head buried in his hands. Tim had been hired to protect Minerva and that was what he was going to do—even if the shots had already been fired. Even if she was already dead.

"Get down!" he shouted.

He lunged forward and I guessed that he meant to throw himself on top of Minerva— which, I had to admit, was quite an attractive idea. Unfortunately, Minerva had already stepped aside. Tim missed and landed, with his arms outstretched, on the red button.

At once, ten thousand lightbulbs burst into multicolored life. This year the Regent Street lights had been sponsored by McDonald's. They depicted stars and Christmas trees decorated with twinkling hamburgers and fries. At the same time a specially arranged Christmas carol—"We Wish You a McMerry Christmas"—boomed out of the speakers.

The mayor opened one eye. "You idiot!" he screamed. "You've turned on the Christmas lights instead of Minerva!"

I'm not sure what would have happened next. Perhaps Tim would have ended up being murdered himself. But then Harold Chase stepped forward and pointed. "There!" he yelled. "There he is!"

He was pointing at the rooftops and now, with all the extra bulbs burning below, the darkness had become a sea of red and blue and yellow and white. And sure enough, high above one of the department stores, I could make out a short, plump figure half hidden behind a chimney stack. He was staring down at us, and although I couldn't see what it was from this distance, there was definitely something in his hand. A gun? He certainly would have had a clear shot at Minerva from where he was standing—but not anymore. Half a dozen policemen had already reached the platform and they had all grabbed a piece of her. Jake and Harold were also grabbing at her. Tim had crawled off the red button and was trying to climb on top. The entire platform looked like practice for a football team with Minerva in the middle of the huddle.

The figure on the roof didn't seem to be moving and that was when I decided to take action. I didn't really know what I was doing.

Part of me was asking questions. Why hadn't I seen the sniper earlier? Why hadn't he made a faster escape—or at least tried to fire off a few more shots? Was that a gun in his hand? And part of me knew that I wouldn't find the answers hanging around on Regent Street. I had to go and look for them myself.

I leaped down from the platform, pushed my way through what was left of the crowd, and plunged into the nearest store. It was a huge place selling clothes that I couldn't possibly afford and—one glance told me—that I wouldn't want to buy if I could. Blue blazers and red ties have never been my style. There was an elevator opposite the front door and I was lucky. The doors were just closing as I arrived. I ran in and pressed the top button—the seventh floor. I was lucky again. The elevator didn't stop on the way up.

The seventh floor seemed to be devoted to Christmas presents for people you don't like: really nasty golf sweaters, oversize umbrellas, and multicolored shoes. There weren't too many shoppers around as I burst out of the elevator and made for the nearest fire exit. Sure enough, a flight of concrete stairs led up to the roof. I took them two at a time and it only occurred to me now that I was unarmed and about to come face-to-face with a would-be assassin who probably wouldn't be too pleased to see me. But it was too late to go back. And, I figured, he couldn't be more deadly than those golf sweaters.

I reached a door marked FIRE EXIT and slammed into it . . . which, incidentally, set off all the fire alarms and the sprinkler system on the seven floors below. But now I was on the roof: a strange landscape of chimneys, satellite dishes, water tanks, and air-conditioning units. I stopped for a moment and let my eyes get used to the darkness. Not that it was exactly pitch-black. The Regent Street lights were still glittering below me, and looking down, I could see the scattered crowds, the police, what was left of the Salvation Army band.

Something moved. And there he was, the man that Harold Chase had seen from below. He was only about fifty feet away from me, cowering on the other side of the roof. He didn't look like your typical assassin. He was short and very fat—almost spherical—with white, curly hair. I wondered if he was one of the overweight Albanians. It was Minerva's absence at a concert in Albania that had started all this.

The man looked at me with something between horror and dismay. He raised a hand as if to prevent me from moving forward.

"No!" he shouted. "I d-d-didn't . . ."

Then he turned and ran.

I chased after him and that was when I discovered that I had miscalculated. I had run into the wrong store and there was a ten-foot gap between his roof and mine. But I hadn't come this far to let an impossible jump and a probable fall to my death seven floors below worry me. I picked up speed and threw myself off the edge.

For a moment I hung in the air and I could feel the ground a very long way beneath me. The cold night air was rushing into me and—for a nasty moment—so was the pavement. The other roof was too far away. I wasn't going to make it. Suddenly I was angry with myself. Who did I think I was? Spider-Man? If so, I'd forgotten to pack a web.

But I didn't fall. Somehow my outstretched hands caught hold of the edge of the other roof and I winced as my stomach and shoulders slammed into the brickwork. I could taste blood and dust in my mouth. I'd cut my lip and maybe loosened a couple of my teeth. Using what little strength I had left, I managed to pull myself up and roll to safety. Painfully, I got to my feet. I wasn't surprised to see that the little fat man had gone.

He had left something behind. I saw them— three small silver objects on the asphalt. At first I thought they were bullets, but as I walked toward them, I realized they were too big. People down in the street were pointing up at me and shouting as I dropped to one knee and scooped them into my hand.

Three oak leaves. That was what the sniper had left behind. The acorn in the cracker and now this. He was definitely trying to tell me something and I'd gotten the message loud and clear.

DINNER FOR TWO

When I woke up the next morning, we were right back where we'd started. Which is to say, we were in Camden Town, in the office, and once again Tim was out of work. It turned out that nobody had been particularly impressed by my death-defying leap when all I had to show for it was grazed arms, bruises, and a handful of silver oak leaves. I'd given the police a description of the man I'd seen on the roof—not that it added up to much. Small and fat. The curly hair could have been a wig. And although he had spoken, he hadn't said enough for me to be sure whether he had an Albanian accent or not.

As I'd sat in the bath that night, I'd gone over his words a dozen times. *No! I d-d-didn't* . . . Had he been scared or did he always stammer like that? And what had he meant? The police had decided that he was angry—that he was telling me he hadn't shot Minerva in the sense that he had missed. To me it seemed simpler than that. "I didn't do it. It wasn't me." That was what he had been trying to say. But then why had he left the oak leaves behind? Maybe they were the symbol of the society for Overweight Albanian Kids. And finally, where was the gun? I thought I'd seen something in his hand, but he hadn't had it when I reached the roof.

Anyway, the case was over as far as we were concerned. Now that the police knew Minerva was in real danger, they had taken over protection duties—and looking at some of those officers leering at her on Regent Street, I could see that plenty of them were going to be putting in for overtime. The good news was that we still had about seventy dollars of the two hundred Jake Hammill had given us. That would buy us a Christmas turkey, brussels sprouts, roast potatoes, and chestnut stuffing. It was just a shame that Tim had sold the oven.

I found him at breakfast with a bowl of cornflakes and the morning newspaper. He wasn't looking too pleased and I soon saw why. He'd made the front page. There was a picture of him spread out on his stomach just after he had accidentally turned on the Christmas lights.

"Have you seen this?" he wailed as I sat down. "And look at this!"

He tapped the caption underneath the picture:

DIM DIAMOND ASSAULTS MAYOR AND TURNS ON THE LIGHTS

"It must be a misprint," he said.

"Are you sure?" I asked.

Tim sighed—and suddenly he was looking sad. "You know, Nick," he began. "Recently, I've been thinking."

"Did it hurt?" I muttered.

He ignored me. "Maybe I should think about getting another job. I mean, look at me! I'm twenty-eight. I never have any money. I'm six months behind on the rent. I can't remember the last time you and I had a square meal."

"We had pizza the night before last," I reminded him.

"That was circular. And whenever I do get a job—like this business with Miranda—it always seems to go wrong." He sighed again. "She told me I was the most stupid person she'd ever met."

"Maybe she was joking."

"She spat at me and tried to strangle me!"

"Well . . . she's Greek."

Tim shook his head. "As soon as the new year begins, I'm going to find myself a proper job," he said. "It shouldn't be too difficult. I've got qualifications."

I fell silent. I didn't have the heart to remind him that he had only taken two courses after high school—and one of them was in embroidery.

It looked as if we were going to have a pretty glum Christmas. But as you'll probably know by now, nothing in our lives ever turns out quite how we expect. A second later there was a knock at the door, and before either of us could react, Minerva walked in. I was so surprised I almost fell off my chair. Tim was so surprised he actually did fall off his.

She was on her own and she was trying to look inconspicuous, dressed in jeans and a black jersey with a thousand-dollar pair of sunglasses hiding her eyes. But Minerva was Minerva. She couldn't look inconspicuous if she covered herself in mud and sat in a swamp.

"Minerva!" Tim gasped as he picked himself up.

"I didn't want to see you," Minerva said, taking off her sunglasses so she could see him better. "I didn't want to come here," she went on. "But I had to. Last night I behaved like a cow."

"You ate grass?" Tim asked.

"No. I behaved disgracefully toward you. I

spat at you. I tried to strangle you. But this morning, when I woke up, I realized I'd gotten it all wrong." She sat down. "Harold brought in the newspapers and I saw that we made every single front page. And part of that was thanks to you. The *Times* called you a maniac. The *Mail* said you were idiotic. The *Guardian* thought you were a banker."

"That *was* a misprint," I said.

Minerva ignored me. "If I'd just turned on those ridiculous lights, the most I would have gotten would have been the front page of the evening paper. But the way things turned out, I got more publicity than I could have dreamed of. Harold is certain my new CD is going to go straight to number one."

"How is Harold?" I asked.

"He had a very lucky escape last night," Minerva said. "One of those bullets missed him by less than an inch. It even burned a hole in the side of his coat."

"You mean . . . it could have hit his pacemaker?" I exclaimed.

"It was a near miss. But I'm not here to talk

about Harold." She turned to Tim. "I want to make it up to you, Timothy," she said. "I want to invite you to dinner. I've already reserved a table for two."

"Isn't two a little early for dinner?" Tim asked.

"For just the two of us, I mean!" Minerva smiled but I wasn't entirely convinced. I'd met sharks with friendlier teeth. "At eight o'clock this evening," she went on. "There's a restaurant I go to. It's called The Gravy." She giggled mischievously. "I thought we might have a little tête-à-tête."

"I'm not that crazy about French food," Tim muttered.

"You will like this." Minerva simpered. "Make sure you dress up. You should put on that suit of yours with seven buttons and seventeen buttonholes."

And with that she was gone.

I went over to the window and looked out as she left the building. There was a police car waiting for her. It was true, then. The men in blue had now taken over Tim's job.

"They're giving her round-the-clock protection," I said.

"They think someone's going to kill her near a clock?"

Tim looked slightly dazed. I could see that he was already imagining himself in some swanky restaurant, drinking champagne with the rich and famous. It was time to bring him down to earth.

"You're not going," I said.

"Why not?" Tim replied.

"She's not interested in you, Tim. If she's invited you out, it's only for the publicity. That's all she cares about."

"Maybe she's got a soft spot for me."

"I don't think she's got a soft spot for anyone except herself. Anyway, she's a married woman."

"Listen, kid." Tim leaned back in his chair. "You don't understand the female mind. Maybe she's looking for something rough and a little bit dangerous."

"Then she can buy herself a yak."

"She likes me!"

"She's using you, Tim."

"She's invited me to dinner!"

"Well, if you're going, I'm going too."

Tim stared at me as if I'd just slapped him in the face—and I can't say I wasn't tempted. "Forget it, Nick," he said. "You heard what she said. This is a dinner for two. I don't need you there. I'm going on my own. And this time, my decision is final!"

The Gravy was one of London's most exclusive restaurants, reserved for celebrities and millionaires. It was so exclusive, even the waiters had trouble getting in, and the name was written in tiny letters as if it didn't want anyone to notice. It was tucked away in a quiet street near Covent Garden with a doorman sizing up everyone who came close. He looked at Tim and me with an expression of complete disgust. But this was the sort of place where even the doormat didn't say WELCOME. It preferred to say GO AWAY.

Why had I come? Part of the answer was that I was worried about Tim. I still didn't know what Minerva was up to, but I didn't trust her and I wanted to be there if things took a turn for the worse. But also, I quite fancied dinner at The Gravy. The food was said to be so good that the chef actually cried when you ate it. The house specialty was leg of lamb cooked in Armagnac—and no matter that it cost you an Armagnac and a leg. Even a glass of water at The Gravy was expensive. It probably came out of a gold-plated tap.

The headwaiter showed us to the best table, and there was Minerva looking stunning in a white silk dress that hugged her tight in all the right places and tighter still in some of the wrong ones. Her face fell when she saw me, but she didn't protest as a couple of waiters hastily added a third setting to the table. It was only as we sat down that she muttered, "I'm surprised you brought your little brother, Timothy. Couldn't you find a babysitter?"

"I'm no baby, Minerva," I said.

"I was hoping to be alone with your big brother. I want to get to know him a little better."

"Just pretend I'm not here."

And that's exactly what she tried to do for the rest of the meal. The waiter came over with three menus, but she chose only for the two of them, leaving me to decide for myself. That suited me. I went for the straightforward steak and potatoes, leaving the fancy stuff with the French names to her and Tim. If I've got one rule in life, it's never eat anything you can't translate.

"So tell me, Timothy," Minerva said, winking at him. "How would you like a little bubbly?"

Tim looked awkward. "Actually, I had a bath before I came."

"Bollinger!" she exclaimed.

"No. Really. I did!"

Minerva ordered a bottle of Bollinger. I asked for a Coke. The way she was making eyes at Tim, it really did seem that she had designs on him and I couldn't understand it. I mean, he was fifteen years younger than her and about fifty thousand times poorer. What could she see in him? I watched him as he opened the champagne for her. There was an explosive pop, followed by a scream from the other side of the room.

"The headwaiter?" Tim asked.

"No," I said. "Just a waiter's head."

Minerva didn't seem to mind. She snuggled up close to him. "I love a man who makes me laugh," she said. "Can I ask you something, Timothy? Do you have a girlfriend?"

"Not at the moment," Tim answered.

"There's nobody waiting for you in bed tonight?"

"It's just Tim and his Paddington Bear hot-water bottle," I told her.

Tim glared at me.

"I fill it for him every night."

The waiter arrived with the first course: soup for me, caviar for Tim and Minerva. Personally, I've never understood caviar. I mean, when I order eggs, I don't expect them to turn up tiny, black, and fifty bucks a mouthful. But Minerva seemed happy enough. I wondered who would pick up the bill.

I could see that Tim was already well out of his depth. He was looking more and more uncomfortable the closer Minerva got, and she was already close enough. Any closer and she would be in his lap.

"Timothy . . . I think you and I were meant for each other," she breathed.

"What about your husband?" Tim squeaked.

She sniffed. "Let's not talk about Harold. He's half the man you are."

"Which half are you talking about?"

I couldn't help butting in again. "If you dislike him so much," I asked, "why did you marry him?"

To my surprise, Minerva looked me in the eye for the first time and I knew at once that she was going to be completely honest. "Why do you think?" she replied coldly. "I married Harold for his money. That was at the start of my career. I'd just left Athens and I had nothing. He promised to help me—and he did. Of course all that's changed now. Now I'm worth millions!"

"So why are you still with him?"

"I can't be bothered to divorce him. Anyway, it's more fun the way things are."

"Does he know where you are tonight?"

Minerva laughed. "Of course he knows. You should have seen his face when I told him I was going out with Timothy. I thought he was going to have a heart attack!"

So that was why she had invited Tim to The Gravy. I should have seen it from the start. Minerva loathed her husband—that much had been obvious when we first met them at their suite at the hotel—and she amused herself by humiliating him. And what better way than to be seen out in public with someone like my big brother, Tim?

At that moment I disliked her as much as anyone I had ever known. More than Charon, the four-fingered assassin we met in Amsterdam. More than my homicidal French teacher, Monsieur Palis. The thing about Minerva was that she was beautiful, rich, and loved by millions. But she had the heart of a snake.

Somehow we got through to the next course. My steak was fine, but I didn't like the look of the gray, jellylike dish that Minerva had ordered for herself and Tim. It came in a yellow sauce with rice and beans.

Tim wasn't sure either. He had eaten about

half of it when he stopped and looked up. "What did you say this was?" he asked.

"Cervelles de veaux au beurre."

He took another mouthful. "It tastes interesting," he said. "What does that mean?"

"Grilled calves' brains in butter."

Two minutes later we were standing outside on the pavement with the doorman glowering at us, glad to see us go.

"That was a nice evening," I said.

"Do you think Minerva enjoyed it?" Tim asked.

"Well, you may have spoiled it a bit when you threw up on her." I looked around for a bus or a taxi.

"I want to go home," Tim groaned. He was still looking very green.

"To Paddington Bear?"

"Just get us a cab!"

But as it turned out, we weren't going to need a bus or a cab. Because just then a car came screeching to a halt in front of us and two men leaped out.

"It's a police car!" Tim exclaimed.

That was particularly brilliant of him and I wasn't sure how he'd worked it out. Maybe it was the blue uniforms the men were wearing. Or it could have been the car with its flashing lights and the word POLICE emblazoned on the side. But he was right. I thought they'd come to look after Minerva—but it was the two of us they headed for.

"Are you Tim Diamond?" one of them asked.

"Yes . . ."

"Get in the car. You're coming down to the station."

"What's going on?" I demanded. "What's happened? And how did you know we were here?"

They ignored me.

The policeman was examining Tim. "We want to talk to you," he said.

"What about?" Tim quavered.

The policeman smiled but without a shred of warmth or humor. It was the sort of smile a doctor might give you before he explained you only had a week to live. "You're wanted, Mr. Diamond," he said. "For murder."

THE DEAD MAN

I don't like police stations. They're full of violent and dangerous characters who need to be kept away from modern society . . . and I'm not talking about the crooks. A lot of people say the British police are wonderful, but I'd have to disagree. I was only fourteen, but I had been arrested so often, it couldn't be long before they gave me my own set of personalized handcuffs. I even spent a month in prison once—and I hadn't done anything wrong! When I look back on it, there's only one word to describe the way I've been treated. Criminal.

This time they drove us to a police station

in Holborn, about ten minutes' drive from
The Gravy. Tim had gone very pale and quiet
in the back of the car. *Cervelles de veaux au
beurre* and now this! We stopped and the two
policemen led us in through a door and down
the usual corridor with white tiles on the walls
and hard neon lighting above . . . the sort of
corridor that can only take you somewhere
you don't want to be. There was an interroga-
tion room at the end: four chairs, one table,
and two detectives. The furniture was hard
and unattractive, but that was nothing com-
pared to the men.

Detective Chief Inspector Snape and Detective Superintendent Boyle. They were old
friends, and like most of Tim's old friends,
they hated us. Why was it that whenever we
got into trouble, the two of them always
seemed to show up? Surely the Metropolitan
Police could have found two new officers to
molest us? Anyway, put an ape and a rott-
weiler in suits and you'll get a rough idea of
Snape and Boyle. Snape was the older of the
two and the one less likely to have rabies. He

was looking old, I thought. But he'd probably looked old the day he was born.

"Well, this really is the perfect end to a horrible day," Snape began as we sat down. It didn't look as if he was going to offer us a cup of tea. "Tim Diamond! The only detective in London with no brains."

Tim went a little green.

"I wouldn't mention brains unless you know a good dry cleaner," I said.

"I want to go to bed!" Tim moaned.

"You're not going anywhere, Diamond," Snape cut in. "I'm investigating a murder and right now you're my only suspect."

"Can I hit him?" Boyle asked hopefully.

"No, Boyle."

"Can I hit his little brother?"

"No!"

"But they were resisting arrest, sir!"

"We haven't arrested them yet, Boyle." Snape shook his head and sighed. "I've just sent Boyle to an anger-management course," he told us.

"Did it work?" I asked.

"No. He got angry and hit the manager, so they sent him back again."

"Well you're wasting your time," I said. "We haven't murdered anyone."

Snape looked at me with disdain. "What can you tell me about a man called Reginald Parker?" he said.

"I can't tell you anything, Snape," I said. "We've never met him."

"What's happened to him?" Tim asked.

"He's been murdered," Snape replied. "He was strangled this afternoon. He lived at Twenty-seven Sparrow Lane and his neighbor heard the sound of a fight. She called us and we found the body."

"What makes you think it's got anything to do with us?" I asked.

Snape nodded at Boyle. "Show them!"

Boyle leaned down and produced a car battery connected to a tangle of wires with clamps on the end. He placed it on the table and glanced unpleasantly at Tim. Snape raised his eyes. "I don't mean that! I want you to show them the evidence!"

Boyle scowled. He opened a drawer and

this time he produced a transparent evidence bag with something inside it. I recognized it at once. *No problem too problematic*. It was Tim's business card.

"We found this next to the body," Snape said. "How do you explain that?"

"A coincidence?" Tim suggested.

Snape's face darkened. "Of course it's not a coincidence, you idiot! It's a clue! Was this Reginald Parker a client of yours? That wouldn't surprise me. Anyone stupid enough to hire you would almost certainly wind up dead."

I shook my head. "I told you, Chief Inspector. We've never seen him."

"How can you be so sure of that? I haven't even told you what he looked like."

Boyle opened the drawer a second time and produced a black-and-white photograph.

You can always tell when the police have taken a picture of someone after they're dead. They don't smile for the camera. In fact, they don't do anything. And the black and the white somehow seems to suit them. All the color has already gone. The photograph showed a short, plump man with curly hair, lying on his back in the mess that had once been the room where he lived. I gasped. Because the truth was that I did know him. I had seen him once and only briefly, but it wasn't a face I was going to forget.

Reginald Parker was the man who had tried to shoot Minerva. He was the man on the roof above Regent Street.

"Did you find a gun in his room?" I asked.

Snape shook his head. "No. I told you. He was strangled."

"How about a handful of silver acorns? Or anything to do with oak trees?"

Boyle leaned over the table and grabbed me by the collar. I felt myself being dragged to my feet. My feet left the floor. One of my shirt buttons went shooting over my shoulder. "Are you making fun of me?" he demanded.

"No!" I gurgled. "I'm trying to help you. I did meet this man. I just didn't know his name."

Boyle turned to Snape, still holding me in the air. "Shall I hook him up to the car battery, sir?"

"Certainly not, Boyle!" Snape looked of-

fended. "He's going to tell us everything anyway."

"I know that, sir. But this way he'll tell us
quicker."

"Just put him down!"

Boyle looked like he was on the verge of
tears, but he dropped me back into my seat.
And then I told them everything that had happened since Jake Hammill had walked into
our office. The meeting at the hotel. The
events in Regent Street. Snape nodded when I
talked about that. He must have seen Tim on
the news.

"You're sure it was Parker on the roof?" he
asked.

"It's the same face, Chief Inspector," I said.

"And you think he was a member of this
organization—Overweight Albanian Kids?"

"He was certainly overweight." I nodded at
the photograph.

"But as far as we know, he wasn't Albanian."

"Maybe he lived in Albania when he was
young."

"We'll check it out."

"Does this mean you're letting us go?" Tim asked, getting to his feet.

"Not so fast, Diamond!"

"All right." Tim sat down, then got up more slowly.

Snape glowered. "I'll see you two again!" he said.

"Yeah. And I'll be waiting." Boyle was standing there holding one of the electrical contacts in his hand. The other was on the table. I passed it to him.

"Don't forget this," I said.

He took it in the other hand.

We could still hear Boyle screaming as we raced back down the corridor and out onto the street. But that's the modern police for you. Shocking.

When Tim and I had breakfast the next morning, I could see he was deep in thought. He didn't even react when he upturned the cereal box and got the plastic toy.

"I just don't get it," he said at length.

"What's that, Tim?"

"Well . . . this guy . . . Archibald Porter."

"I think you mean Reginald Parker."

"He tried to kill Minerva and now somebody has killed him. But that doesn't make any sense. Nobody knew who he was. So why kill him? If they wanted to protect Minerva, they could have just reported him to the police."

He frowned but then his eyes brightened. "Maybe it was just another coincidence!" he exclaimed. "Maybe his death was an accident!"

"It's quite tricky to get strangled by accident," I pointed out.

Tim nodded. "I wonder how he got my business card?"

"That's exactly what we're going to find out . . ."

We were lucky that Snape had given us Parker's address. As soon as Tim had finished breakfast, we looked up Sparrow Lane on Tim's map of London. Then we took a bus to the other side of London and a narrow street of terraced houses not far from the old meat market. Number 27 was halfway down and looked exactly the same as numbers 25 and 29—apart, that is, from the policeman on duty and the blue-and-white POLICE LINE: DO NOT CROSS taped over the front door.

To be honest, I'd forgotten that Snape would have left someone on duty and I could see at a glance that we weren't going to get past the policeman at the door. He had the sort of face that if he ever decided to join the dog unit, he wouldn't need a dog. Ignoring him, I went straight to the house next door and rang the bell, hoping the owner would be in.

She was. The door opened and a huge, cheerful Caribbean woman in a brilliantly colored dress appeared on the doorstep, the great slabs that were arms folded across her ample breasts. "Yes, me darlings? How can I help you?" she boomed out.

I nudged Tim.

"I'm Tim Diamond," Tim said.

"Yes?" The woman was none the wiser.

"My brother is a private detective," I told her. "He wants to ask you some questions about the guy who lived next door."

"That's right," Tim explained. "And if he lived next door, then I'd imagine he must have been your neighbor."

"That's brilliant, Tim," I muttered. "How did you work that one out?"

It turned out that the woman was called Mrs. Winterbotham and had lived at number 25 for almost as many years. Her husband was out, working at the meat market, and she invited us into her kitchen and gave us tea and coconut cookies. She had already told the police everything, but she was going to enjoy telling us again.

"Reginald was an actor," she said, then looked left and right and lowered her voice as if he might be listening from beyond the grave. "But he wasn't a very good one. Oh no! He was out of work most of the time. He was in *The Cherry Orchard* last May, playing one of the cherries. And last year he appeared at the Unicorn Theatre in a one-man show."

"Was it popular?" I asked.

"No. Only one man came." She dropped three sugar cubes into her tea and helped herself to another cookie. "Reginald was a nice man. But, you know, I'm not sure it really helped his career, his having a stutter."

I remembered now. Parker had stuttered when he was on the roof. So it hadn't been because he was afraid.

"I said to him that he ought to be a mime artist," Mrs. Winterbotham went on. "That way he wouldn't have had to talk. But I don't think people would have paid to see him. He didn't have the figure for it. To be honest with you, I've seen more attractive figures hanging up in the meat market."

"When was his last job?" I asked.

"Well . . ." She put down the cookie and leaned forward conspiratorially. "That's what I told the police. He always got a job at Christmas. He worked in a department store. But this year something very unusual happened. He got paid for a one-night appearance in the West End! He didn't tell me what it was, but I do know that it was a lot of money."

"Who paid him?"

"He never said. But I don't think it can have worked out because when I saw him the next morning, he was very upset."

"How do you know he was upset?" Tim asked.

"He was crying."

"You're sure they weren't tears of happiness?"

"Oh no, Mr. Diamond. He was completely miserable. And then that afternoon, someone came to the house. I heard this banging and crashing and I went out to the yard to see what was happening. Then there was silence. I knocked on the door but I got no answer. So I called the police."

"Just one last question for you, Mrs. Winterbotham . . ." I began.

"Please. Call me Janey!"

"Was Reginald Parker Albanian?"

"No. As far as I know, he'd never been to Albania. In fact, he never went anywhere. He couldn't afford it. Most of the time he just sat at home and watched TV." She sighed and I got the idea that maybe she'd been his only friend in the world. "And now he's dead. I can't believe it. Now, how about a nice piece of banana cake?"

We didn't have the cake.

Because suddenly, even as Mrs. Winterbotham had been talking, everything had made sense. Suddenly I was back on the roof, hearing Reginald Parker as he called out across the gap. *I d-d-didn't* . . . I saw the cracker with the acorn and the death threat and knew what it was that was wrong with the letter Minerva had been sent. I thought about Regent Street and the bullet that had come so close it had drilled a hole in Harold Chase's coat. I knew exactly what job Reginald had been hired for—it could only be one job—and I also knew what was going to happen at twelve o'clock that day. I looked at my watch. It was five past eleven. We had less than one hour left.

"We have to get to Harrods, Tim!" I said.

Tim shook his head. "This is no time for Christmas shopping, Nick."

"We're not going shopping. We have to find Minerva."

"Why?"

A taxi drove by. I reached out and flagged it down.

"She's going to be murdered, Tim. And I know who by."

KILLER WITH A SMILE

We were on the wrong side of town. We had to cross all of London to reach Knightsbridge, and with Christmas just weeks away, the traffic could hardly be worse. As we sat in a traffic jam on the edge of Hyde Park, I could feel the minutes ticking away. Worse than that, I could see them. The taxi meter was running and Tim was staring at it in dismay, watching as the last of his earnings disappeared.

We finally made it with about five minutes and ten bucks to spare, but even so it was going to be tight. Harrods was a huge place and the workshop was right up on the fourth floor. Worse than that, the entire store was heaving—not just with shoppers but with the usual crowd of fans and policemen who had turned out to see or to protect Minerva. There were security men on all the doors and more photographers waiting in the street, although you'd have thought by now the papers would have had enough of her. I certainly had.

And what nobody knew was that the killer was already inside the building. He would smile at Minerva and he would murder her . . . and she wouldn't even know it had happened until she woke up dead.

"This way, Tim!"

We had plunged off the street and into women's handbags, then into cosmetics, then food. Harrods was every Christmas present you could ever imagine—more presents than anyone in the world could ever want. It was Christmas gone mad: hundreds of miles of tinsel; thousands of glittering stars and balls; enough Christmas trees to repopulate a forest. Don't get me wrong. I love Christmas and I'll tear open as many presents as I can get my hands on. But as I ran for the escalators, past the groaning shelves and the grinning sales-clerks, I couldn't help but feel there had to be something more to it than this. Maybe something less, if you know what I mean.

We reached the escalators and began to fight our way up. I had a strange sense of déjà vu as I went. Suddenly I was in another department store in a different part of London almost two years before. I'd been running then too—to escape from two German assassins who'd been trying to make sure that the only way I saw Boxing Day was from inside a box. But that was another time and another story, and if you want to know about it, I'm afraid you're going to have to buy another book.

We got to the fourth floor and there was a sign pointing toward Santa's workshop, "Jingle Bells" blaring out of the speakers and little kids everywhere, dragging their mothers to see the man in red.

I stopped, panting. "I hope we're not too late," I gasped.

"Yes," Tim agreed. "Santa may not have any presents left!"

Sometimes I think Tim doesn't belong in the real world. Maybe he'd be more comfortable in a nice white room with padded walls. But this was no time to argue. It was twelve noon exactly. Somewhere in the clock department down below, a thousand clocks would be chiming, bleeping, or shooting out cuckoos. The workshop had just been opened by Minerva. And the way ahead was blocked.

There were toys everywhere. Vast LEGO castles, cuddly toys, jigsaw mountains, and Scalextric slot cars buzzing around in furious circles. Children were pulling and pushing in every direction. In the far distance I could see the green plastic entrance to a green plastic cave with a long line of people waiting to go in. That was where we had to be. But our path had been closed off by a three-hundred-pound store security guard with the body of a wrestler and the face of a boxer at the end of a particularly vicious fight. At least I assumed he was a security guard. It was hard to be sure. He was dressed as an elf.

"You can't go this way!" he told me. "You

have to go to the back of the line." So he *was* a security guard. I should have known. How many elves do you see carrying nightsticks?

"Where's Minerva?" I demanded. I was afraid I was already too late—and this brute in green tights was only making things worse.

"She's in with Santa Claus, opening the workshop. You'll have to wait in line if you want her autograph."

"I don't want her autograph. I want to save her life!"

But it was no good. I might as well have argued with Rudolph the Red-Nosed Reindeer (there was a mechanical version next to the workshop). I had to stop myself from pulling out my hair. I was expecting a gunshot at any moment and here I was trying to reason with an elf. I looked around me, wondering if I could bribe him with a cuddly toy—or if not, hit him with one. That was when I saw Detective Chief Inspector Snape, standing grim-faced with Boyle next to him, the two of them surrounded by Barbie dolls.

"Snape!" I shouted out, and before the

security guard could stop me, I had run over to the two men.

"What are you doing here, Diamond?" he snapped the moment he saw me.

Boyle curled his lip and looked ugly—which in his case wasn't very difficult. Once again he lumbered forward and grabbed hold of me.

"Don't worry, Boyle!" I said. "I haven't come here to steal your Barbie doll."

"Then why are you here?" Snape demanded.

"You've got to find Minerva," I began. "She's in danger."

"I know she's in danger," Snape replied. "Boyle and I are on special duty. We're looking after her."

"You don't understand . . ."

How could I tell them what I knew? There wasn't enough time, and with all the noise in the place—the children screaming, the music playing, Rudolph singing and all the rest of it—I'd have been hoarse before I got to the end. But just then Minerva appeared, coming out of the workshop with her manager, Jake

Hammill, next to her. There was no sign of her husband, but somehow I wasn't surprised.

I twisted out of Boyle's grip, and with Tim right behind me I ran over to her. As usual, Minerva was looking drop-dead gorgeous in a slinky, silver number, and despite everything, I was glad that I had arrived in time and that she hadn't, after all, dropped dead. She was holding a present, about the size and shape of a shoe box. Santa must have just given it to her.

She saw me. "You!" she snapped—and unless that's Greek for Happy Christmas, she wasn't too pleased to see me.

I stood in front of her, my eyes fixed on the box. I didn't want to touch it. To be honest, I didn't want to be anywhere near it. I had a good idea what was inside.

"Did Santa give you that?" I demanded.

"Yes." She nodded.

"Do you know what it is?"

Minerva shrugged. She didn't really care. She was only here for the publicity. "No," she said.

"I think it's a clock," Tim chimed in.

"Why?"

"Well . . . I can hear it ticking."

Snape leaned forward and took the box. "What's all this about?" he demanded.

"Chief Inspector," I said, and suddenly my mouth was dry. "I'd be very careful with that unless you want to spend this Christmas in six different parts of London all at the same time."

"What are you talking about?" Hammill demanded.

"There's probably an oak leaf or two in there and maybe some acorns. But I'll bet you any money that the rest of it is a bomb."

Maybe I said the word too loudly. Somehow the crowd caught on to what was happening and suddenly the entire department was filled with hysterical mothers dragging their screaming kids off to the nearest escalator. I ignored them. I just wanted to know if Snape was going to believe me. And to be fair to him, just this once he gave me the benefit of the doubt. Very gently, he lowered the box to the ground, then turned to Boyle. "Have you got a knife?" he asked.

Boyle reached into his pocket and took out first a cutthroat razor, then a bayonet, and finally a switchblade. He pressed a button and six inches of ugly steel leaped out to join in the cheerful Christmas atmosphere. Snape took it. Very carefully, he cut a square in the side of the parcel and peeled the cardboard back. He looked inside.

"He's right!" he said.

He didn't need to tell me. Looking over his shoulder, I could just make out part of an alarm clock, some loops of wire, and something that could have been modeling clay but definitely wasn't.

Snape looked up. "Plastic explosive," he whispered. "It's connected to an alarm clock. It'll blow up when the bell goes." He squinted through the square he had cut out. Then, very slowly, he handed the package to Boyle. "All right, Boyle," he said. "This is timed to go off in forty minutes. You'd better get it down to the bomb disposal squad."

"Where's that?" I asked.

"It's a forty-five-minute drive away."

Boyle stared at him.

"See if you can find a shortcut," Snape advised.

Boyle disappeared—in a hurry. Snape turned to me. "So what's this all about?" he demanded.

"Santa just gave me that!" Minerva rasped. She was standing there dazed.

"Have you been a bad girl this year?" Tim asked.

"It's not Santa!" I said. "Come on . . ."

The five of us—me, Tim, Minerva, Jake Hammill, and Snape—dived into the workshop. Out of the corner of my eye I saw the security guard talking into his radio, presumably calling for reinforcements. There was nobody else left on the fourth floor—as far as I knew, there was nobody left in Knightsbridge. White plastic snow crunched underfoot as we followed the path into the workshop. White plastic stalactites hung down and white plastic stalagmites pointed up—or maybe it was the other way around. I can never remember. We passed a couple more mechanical singing reindeer and arrived just in time to see a familiar red figure, about to leave by a back exit.

"Hold it right there, Santa!" I shouted.

Santa froze, then slowly turned around.

"It's . . . it's . . . it's . . . !" Tim exclaimed. He stopped. He had no idea who it was, and with the red hood, the white beard, and the golden-framed spectacles, I couldn't blame him. His own mother wouldn't recognize him. His own wife hadn't.

I walked forward and pulled off the beard. And there he was.

"Harold!" Minerva exclaimed.

"Harold?" Hammill quavered.

"That's right," I said. "Harold Chase."

There could be no doubt about it. The old man reached up and lowered the hood, revealing more of his face, his silver hair, and his hearing aid. He had concealed his permanent suntan with makeup. But there could be no disguising the venom with which he was looking at his wife.

Snape took over. "You just gave Minerva a bomb," he said.

Harold Chase said nothing.

"That's a very original present," Tim commented.

"Not really, Tim," I said. "He was trying to kill her."

It was the word *kill* that did it. The bomb had been taken away. But Harold Chase exploded. "I hate her!" he screamed. "You have no idea what it's been like living with her! I know why she married me. She wanted my money! But now that she's so big and so famous she doesn't need me. And so she humiliates and belittles me. She's made my life hell!"

He took a step toward us. Tim took three steps back.

"But that's not the worst of it," Harold went on. "She's a hypocrite. She smiles at the crowds on Regent Street when secretly she despises them. She hates Christmas too—and every year she's ruined it for me. No carols, no presents, no tinsel, no fun. She's stolen Christmas from me and that was a good enough reason to want to see her dead."

By now, he was frothing at the mouth and I almost wished Boyle was there to deal with him. Fortunately the security guard disguised as an elf had appeared with two colleagues, and the three of them dragged Harold out. He was still screaming as he went.

The five of us went back downstairs to a champagne bar on the ground floor. It was somewhere quiet and we had a lot to talk about. Minerva paid for champagne for herself and the others. I got a glass of lemonade. I had to admit she seemed very shaken by what had happened. Her face was pale. Her eyes were thoughtful. And even her silver-plated breasts seemed to have lost their sparkle.

"All right, Diamond," Snape said, emptying his glass. "Spit it out!"

"He hasn't drunk anything yet," Tim said.

"I want you to tell me what's been going on. How did you know about Harold Chase and how did you figure out his plan?"

"I worked it out when we visited Janey Winterbotham," I explained.

"The next-door neighbor?" Snape sniffed. "I spoke to her. She didn't tell me anything."

"She told me that Reginald Parker was an out-of-work actor but that he had a job in a department store every Christmas," I said. "What else could he have been but a department-store Santa? That was when it all fell into place."

"Why don't you start at the beginning?" Jake Hammill suggested.

"All right." I drew a breath. "This is the way I see it. Harold Chase hated Minerva for all the reasons he just told us. His hatred had obviously driven him mad and he decided to kill her. But the trouble was, it was too obvious. If Minerva died, he would be the main suspect. Everyone knew how badly she treated him."

"A lot of people would die to be married to me," Minerva sniffed.

"He *was* married to you—and you were the one he wanted to die," I reminded her. "Anyway, Harold couldn't kill you himself. He'd be arrested at once. But then he had an idea.

He realized that the best way to get rid of you was to create someone who didn't exist: a crazy fan. He used that concert you canceled —for Overweight Albanian Kids—and pretended that someone was out to get revenge."

"You mean . . . it was Harold who wrote that anonymous letter?" Hammill asked.

"Exactly. He even put a fake spelling mistake in it—but if he couldn't spell *forgive*, how come he could spell *forget* a few lines later? The whole thing felt fake to me."

"And what about the cracker?"

"That was another clue. I thought at the time that there was something weird about it, but it was only later that I realized what it was." I turned to Hammill. "You'd booked Minerva into the Porchester Hotel under a false name."

"Right," he said.

"But the box of crackers was addressed to her. Whoever sent it even knew the number of the suite where she was staying. It had to be an inside job."

"But wait a minute," Snape interrupted. "If

it was Chase all the time, what was Reginald Parker doing on the roof at Regent Street?"

"Reginald Parker had been paid by Chase," I explained. "His neighbor told us he got a lot of money for a job in the West End. She probably thought it was a job in theater. My guess is that Chase paid him to leave the silver oak leaves on the roof. Parker had no idea what he was doing. He didn't have a gun or anything. I saw him carrying something, but it could have been a camera. After all, he knew Minerva was there. He was a complete innocent. That's what he tried to tell me when I went up there. 'I didn't . . . ' That was all he managed. But what he wanted to say was, 'I didn't do it!' He must have been horrified when he heard the shots."

"So who *did* shoot at me?" Minerva asked. She poured herself some more champagne. I wondered what she was celebrating. Maybe it was the fact she was still alive.

"That was Harold," I said. "Again, I'm only guessing, but I'd say he fired two blank shots from a gun he had inside his pocket.

When we were on the platform, the shots sounded very close. He fired twice and then pointed to Reginald up on the roof—because, of course, he knew he'd be there. You see, he was creating the illusion of a killer . . . someone who didn't really exist. The only snag is, the gun burned a hole in his coat." I glanced at Minerva. "You thought he'd almost been hit. In fact, he'd fired the shots himself."

"I don't get it," Minerva exclaimed. "He wanted to protect me! It was Harold who persuaded me to get a bodyguard!"

"He did that to throw off any suspicion. At the same time he made sure you hired the worst private detective in London. Someone too stupid to get in the way of his plan."

"And who was that?" Tim asked.

"Have some more champagne, Tim," I said.

"And then Harold Chase killed Reginald Parker," Snape said.

"You've got it in one, Chief Inspector. Chase had chosen Parker because he knew he was going to be the Santa Claus at Harrods. First of all he hired him to go on the roof.

Then he killed him and took his place. Tim's business card must have fallen out of his pocket during the fight. It was when I saw the card that I put two and two together . . ."

"You did your math homework?" Tim asked.

"No, Tim. I cracked the case."

There was a long silence. Either I'd been talking too slowly or they'd been drinking too quickly, but all the champagne was gone. And I hadn't even touched my lemonade.

Jake Hammill put an arm around Minerva. "Baby, I'm so sorry," he said. "What a terrible experience for you!"

Minerva shrugged. "It wasn't so bad," she said. "I've gotten rid of Harold. I'm going to get lots of publicity. And my CD's certain to go to number one." She got to her feet. I thought she was going to leave, but she took one last look at me. "You're quite smart for a scruffy fourteen-year-old," she said. Then she flicked her eyes toward Tim. "As for you, you're just an utter loss."

She walked out.

"What did she mean?" Tim wailed.

I thought for a moment. "Justanutterloss. It's Greek for sensational," I said.

"Really?" Tim's eyes lit up.

"Sure, Tim," I said. Well, after all, it was Christmas.

EPILOGUE

There are a few things to add.

Two weeks later, Tim and I got a surprise in the mail—and this time it wasn't a bomb, an unpaid bill, or a poison-pen letter. It was a note from Jake Hammill. It seemed that he wasn't so bad after all. We had just saved his most famous client from a murder attempt that would have been not only the end of her career, but—even worse—the end of his percentage. And as a token of his gratitude, he'd decided to send us a check for ten thousand dollars. I'll never forget the sight of Tim holding it between his hands. The last time he had seen that many zeros, it had been on his report card.

We talked a lot about what to do with the money. Of course we were going to have a proper Christmas lunch. Tim was going to pay the rent. I was finally going to get a new school uniform—the last one had so many patches in it, it was more patches than uniform. But that would still leave us with several thousand, which was just about the most money we'd ever had.

I forget who suggested it first, but that was when we decided to fly out to Australia to be reunited with our parents. It had been years since we'd seen them, and sometimes I thought it was unnatural for a young lad to be living without his mother, often crying himself to sleep, having to be tucked in every night and cheered up by his brother. Not that I minded doing all that for Tim, but even so I thought it would do us all good to be a family again, just for a while.

And the next day we bought two British Airways tickets to Sydney. We were going to travel out as soon as the Easter term ended, and maybe one day I'll write down what actually happened when we got there. *The Radius of the Lost Shark*. That's the title I've got written down in my notebook. It's another story I've got to tell.

What else is there? Harold Chase got life in jail for attempted murder, but looking at him, I didn't think that would be too many years. Snape took the credit for the arrest, of course. They actually put his face on the front cover of the monthly police journal, *Hello, Hello, Hello* magazine. Reginald Parker's remains were scattered in the River Thames, in front of the National Theatre—as he'd requested in his will. It can't have been pleasant, though. He hadn't been cremated.

And what about Minerva? She may have gotten to number one, but I didn't care. I never listened to her music again. She may have had everything, but without a heart you're just nothing. She was like a December without Christmas—and at the end of the day, what's the point of that?

Turn the page for a preview of
the first Diamond Brothers mystery,

THE FALCON'S MALTESER

The Falcon's Malteser

Malteser

A Diamond Brothers Mystery

THE PACKAGE

There's not much call for private detectives in Fulham.

The day it all started was a bad one. Business was so slack it was falling down all around us. The gas had been disconnected that morning, one of the coldest mornings for twenty years, and it could only be a matter of time before the electricity followed. We'd run out of food and the people in the supermarket downstairs had all fallen down laughing when I suggested credit. We had just $2.37 and about three teaspoons of instant coffee to last us the weekend. The wallpaper was peeling, the carpets were fraying, and the curtains . . . well, whichever way you looked at it, it was curtains for us. Even the cockroaches were walking out.

I was just wondering whether the time hadn't finally come to do something constructive—like packing my bags and going back to Mum—when the door opened and the dwarf walked in.

Okay—maybe you're not supposed to call them dwarfs these days. Vertically challenged . . . that's what it says in the book. But not this book. The truth is, this guy was as challenged as they come. I was only thirteen but already I had six inches on him, and the way he looked at me with cold, unforgiving eyes—he knew it and wasn't going to forget it.

He was in his midforties, I guessed. It was hard to say with someone that size. A short, dark stranger with brown eyes and a snub nose. He was wearing a three-piece suit, only the pieces all belonged to different suits like he'd gotten dressed in a hurry. His socks didn't match either. A neat mustache crowned his upper lip and his black hair was slicked back with oil. A spotted bow tie and a flashy gold ring completed the picture. It was a weird picture.

"Do come in, Mr. . . . ." my brother began.

"Naples," the dwarf, who already was in, said. His name might have come out of Italy, but he spoke with a South American accent. "Johnny Naples. You are Tim Diamond?"

"That's me," my brother lied. His real name was Herbert Timothy Simple, but he called himself Tim Diamond. He thought it suited his image. "And what can I do for you, Mr. Venice?"

"Naples," the dwarf corrected him. He climbed onto a chair and sat down opposite my brother. His nose just reached the level of the desk. Herbert slid a paperweight out of the way to give his new client a clear view. The dwarf was about to speak when he paused and the nose turned toward me. "Who is he?" he demanded, the two *h*s scratching at the back of his throat.

"Him?" Herbert smiled. "He's just my kid brother. Don't worry about him, Mr. Navels. Just tell me how I can help you."

Naples laid a carefully manicured hand on the desk. His

initials—JN—were cut into a gleaming ring. There was so much gold around that third finger he could have added his name and address, too. "I want to deposit something with you," he said.

"Deposit?" Herbert repeated quite unnecessarily. The dwarf might have had a thick accent, but it certainly wasn't as thick as my brother. "You mean . . . like in a bank?" he continued, brilliantly.

The dwarf raised his eyes to the ceiling, took in the crack in the plaster, and then, with a sigh, lowered them onto Herbert. "I want to leave a package with you," he said briskly. "It's important you look after it. But you must not open it. Just keep it here and keep it safe."

"For how long?"

Now the dwarf's eyes darted across to the window. He swallowed hard and loosened his bow tie. I could see that he was scared of something or somebody in the street outside. Either that or he had a fear of storm windows.

"I don't know," he replied. "About a week maybe. I'll come back and collect it . . . when I can. You give it to nobody else except for me. You understand?"

Naples pulled out a packet of Turkish cigarettes and lit one. The smoke curled upward, a lurid blue in the chill morning air. My brother flicked a piece of chewing gum toward his mouth. It missed and disappeared over his shoulder.

"What's in the package?" he asked.

"That's my business," the dwarf said.

"Okay. Let's talk about my business, then." Herbert treated his client to one of his "don't mess with me" smiles. It made him look about as menacing as a cow with a stomachache. "I'm not cheap," he went on. "If you want a cheap private eye, try looking in the cemetery. You want me to look after your package? It'll cost you."

The dwarf reached into his jacket pocket and pulled out the first good thing I'd seen that week: fifty portraits of Alexander Hamilton, each one printed in green. In other words, a bundle of ten-dollar bills, brand-new and crisp. "There's five hundred dollars here," he said.

"Five hundred?" Herbert squeaked.

"There will be another five hundred when I return and pick up the package. I take it that is sufficient?"

My brother nodded his head, an insane grin on his face. Put him in the back of a car and who'd need a bobbing-head doll?

"Good." The dwarf stubbed out his half-smoked cigarette and slid off the chair. Then he removed a plain brown envelope from another pocket. It was quite thick with something vaguely rectangular bulging in the center. It rattled faintly as he put it on the desk. "Here is the package," he said. "Once again, look after it, Mr. Diamond. With your life. And whatever you do, don't open it."

"You can trust me, Mr. Nipples," my brother muttered. "Your package is in safe hands." He waved one of the safe hands to illustrate the point, sending a mug of coffee flying.

"What happens if I need to get in touch with you?" he asked as an afterthought.

"You don't," Naples snapped. "I get in touch with you."

"Well, there's no need to be touchy," Herbert said.

It was then that a car in the street backfired. The dwarf seemed to evaporate. One moment he was standing beside the desk. The next he was crouching beneath it, one hand inside his jacket. And somehow I knew that his finger wasn't wrapped round another bundle of money. For about thirty seconds nobody moved. Then Naples slid across to the window, standing to one side so that he could look out without being seen. He had to stand on tiptoe to do it, his hands perched on the sill, the side of his face pressed against the glass. When he turned around, he left a damp circle on the window. Hair oil and sweat.

"I'll see you again in a week," he said. He made for the door as fast as his legs could carry him. With his legs, that wasn't too fast. "Look after that package with your life, Mr. Diamond," he repeated. "And I mean . . . your life."

And then he was gone.

My brother was jubilant. "Five hundred bucks just for looking after an envelope," he crowed. "This is my lucky day. This is the best thing that's happened to me this year." He glanced at the package. "I wonder what's in it?" he murmured. "Still, that shouldn't worry us. As far as we're concerned, there's no problem."

That's what Herbert thought. But right from the start I

wasn't so sure. I mean, five hundred dollars is five hundred dollars, and when you're throwing that sort of money around, there's got to be a good reason. And I remembered the dwarf's face when the car backfired. He may have been a small guy, but he seemed to be expecting big trouble.

Just how big I was to find out soon enough.

TIM DIAMOND INC.

The five hundred dollars lasted about half a day. But it was a good half day.

It began with a blowout at a café round the corner. Double eggs, double sausage, double fries, and fried bread but no beans. We'd been living on beans for the best part of a week. It had gotten so bad I'd been having nightmares about giant Heinz cans chasing me down the High Street.

After that, Herbert put an ad in the local paper for a cleaning lady. That was crazy, really. There was no way we could afford one—but on the other hand, if you'd seen the state of our place, maybe you'd have understood. Dust everywhere, dirty plates piled high in the sink, and old socks sprawled across the carpet from the bedroom to the front door as if they were trying to get to the Laundromat under their own steam. Then we took a bus into the West End. Herbert bought me a new jacket for the next term at school and bought himself some new thermal underwear and a hot-water bottle. That left just about enough money to get two tickets for a film. We went to see *101 Dalmations*. Herbert cried all the way through. He even cried in the coming attractions. That's what sort of guy he is.

I suppose it was pretty strange, the two of us living

together the way we did. It had all happened about two years back when my parents suddenly decided to emigrate to Australia. Herbert was twenty-three then. I'd just turned eleven.

We were living in a comfortable house in a nice part of London. I still remember the address: 1 Wiernotta Mews. My dad worked as a door-to-door salesman. Doors was what he sold; fancy French sliding doors and traditional English doors, pure mahogany, made in Korea. He really loved doors. Ours was the only house in the street with seventeen ways in. As for my mum, she had a part-time job in a pet shop. It was after she got bitten by a rabid parrot that they decided to emigrate. I wasn't exactly wild about the idea, but of course nobody asked me. You know how some parents think they own their kids? Well, I couldn't even sneeze without written permission signed in duplicate.

Neither Herbert nor I really got on with our parents. That was one thing we had in common. Oh yeah . . . and we didn't get on with each other. That was the second thing. He'd just joined the police force (this was one week before the Hendon Police Training Center burned down) and could more or less look after himself, but of course I had as much independence as the coffee table.

"You'll love Australia," my dad said. "It's got kangaroos."

"And boomerangs," my mum added.

"And wonderful, maple-wood doors . . ."

"And koalas."

"I'm not going!" I said.

"You are!" they screamed.

So much for reasoned argument.

I got as far as Heathrow Airport. But just as the plane to Sydney was about to take off, I slipped out the back door and managed to find my way out of the airport. Then I hightailed it back to Fulham. I'm told my mum had hysterics about thirty-five thousand feet above Bangkok. But by then it was too late.

Now, by this time, Herbert had finished with the police force, or to put it more accurately, the police force had finished with Herbert. He'd finally gotten fired for giving someone directions to a bank. I suppose it wasn't his fault that the someone had robbed it, but he really shouldn't have held the door for the guy as he came out. But in the meantime, he'd managed to save up some money and had rented this run-down apartment in the Fulham Road, above a supermarket, planning to set himself up as a private detective. That's what it said on the door:

TIM DIAMOND INC.
PRIVATE DETECTIVE

Inside, you went up a staircase to a glass-fronted door, which in turn led into his office, a long, narrow room with four windows looking out into the street. A second door led off from here into the kitchen. The staircase continued up to a second floor, where we both had a bedroom and shared a bathroom. The apartment had been made available to Herbert at a bargain-basement price, probably because the whole place was so rickety it was threatening to collapse into the basement at any time. The stairs wobbled when you went up and the bath wobbled when you turned on the taps. We never saw the landlord. I think he was afraid to come near the place.

Dark-haired and blue-eyed, Herbert was quite hand-some—at least from the opposite side of the street on a foggy day. But what God had given him in looks, He had taken away in brains. There might have been worse private detectives than Tim Diamond. But somehow I doubt it.

I'll give you an example. His first job was to find some rich lady's pedigree Siamese cat. He managed to run it over on the way to see her. The second job was a divorce case—which you may think is run-of-the-mill until I tell you that the clients were perfectly happily married until he came along.

There hadn't been a third case.

Anyway, Herbert was not overjoyed to see me that day when I turned up from Heathrow carrying a suitcase that held exactly nothing, but where else could I go? We argued. I told him it was a fait accompli. We argued some more. I told him what a fait accompli was. In the end he let me stay.

Mind you, I often wondered if I'd made the right decision. For a start, when I say I like a square meal a day I don't mean a sawed-off shredded wheat, and it's no fun starting the winter term in clothes you grew out of the summer before, with more holes in your socks than a Swiss cheese. We could never afford anything. Her Majesty's government helped Herbert out a little, which is a fancy way of saying that he got welfare, and my parents sent the occasional check for my upkeep, but even so, Herbert never managed to make ends meet. I tried to persuade him to get himself a sensible job—anything other than private detection—but it was hopeless. As hopeless as Herbert himself.

Anyway, after the movie, we got back to the flat around eleven and were making our way up the stairs past the office when Herbert stopped. "Wait a minute, Nick," he said. "Did you leave the door open?"

"No," I said.

"That's strange . . ."

He was right. The door of the office was open, the moon-light pouring out of the crack like someone had spilled a can of silver paint. We made our way back downstairs and went in. I turned on the light.

"Oh dear," my brother said. "I think we've had visitors."

That was the understatement of the year. A stampede of wild bulls would have left the place in better order. The desk had been torn open, the carpets torn up, the bookshelves torn apart, and the curtains torn down. The old filing cabinet would have fit into so many matchboxes. Even the telephone had been demolished, its various parts scattered around the room. Whoever had been there, they'd done a thorough job. If we'd been invited to a wedding, we could have taken the office along for confetti.

"Oh dear," Herbert repeated. He stepped into the rubble

and picked up what was now a very dead cactus. A moment later, he dropped it, his lower jaw falling at about the same speed. "My God!" he shrieked. "The envelope!"

He stumbled over to the remains of his desk and searched in the rubble of the top drawer. "I put it here," he said. He fumbled about on the floor. "It's gone!" he moaned at last. He got back to his feet, clenching and unclenching his fists. "The first job I've had in six months and now I've gone and lost it. You know what this means, don't you? It means we won't get the other five hundred dollars. I'll probably have to pay back the five hundred we've already spent. What a disaster! What a catastrophe! I don't know why I bother, really I don't. It's just not fair!" He gave the desk a great thump with his boot. It groaned and collapsed in a small heap.

Then he looked at me. "Well, don't just stand there," he snapped.

"What am I supposed to do?" I asked.

"Well . . . say something."

"All right," I said. "I didn't think it was a very good idea to leave the package in your desk . . ."

"It's a fat lot of good telling me now," Herbert whined. It looked as though he was going to cry.

"I didn't think it was a good idea," I continued, "so I took it with me." I pulled the envelope out of my jacket pocket, where it had been resting all evening.

My brother seized it and gave it a big wet kiss. He didn't even thank me.

Turn the page for a preview of
the Diamond Brothers mystery,

Public Enemy Number Two

Public Enemy Number Two

A Diamond Brothers Mystery

FRENCH DICTATION

I didn't like Peregrine Palis from the start. It's a strange thing about French teachers. From my experience they all have either dandruff, bad breath, or silly names. Well, Mr. Palis had all three, and when you add to that the fact that he was on the short side, with a potbelly, a hearing aid, and hair on his neck, you'll agree that he'd never win a Mr. Universe contest . . . or a *Combat Monsieur Univers* as he might say.

He'd only been teaching at the school for three months—if you can call his brand of bullying and sarcasm teaching. Personally I've learned more from a stick of French bread. I remember the first day he strutted into the classroom. He never walked. He moved his legs like he'd forgotten they were attached to his waist. His feet came first, with the rest of his body trying to catch up. Anyway, he wrote his name on the blackboard—just the last bit.

"My name is Palis," he said. "Pronounced 'pallee.' P-A-L-I-S."

We all knew at once that we'd gotten a bad one. He hadn't been in the place thirty seconds and already he'd written his name, pronounced it, and spelled it out. The next thing he'd be having it embroidered on our uniforms. From that moment on, things got steadily worse. He'd treat the smallest mistake like a personal insult. If you spelled something wrong, he'd make you write it out fifty times. If you mispronounced a word, he'd say you were torturing the language. Then he'd torture you. Twisted ears were his specialty. What can I say? French genders were a nightmare. French tenses have never been more tense. After a few months of Mr. Palis, I couldn't even look at French doors without breaking into tears.

Things came to a head as far as I was concerned one Tuesday afternoon in the summer term. We were being given dictation and I leaned over and whispered something to a friend. It wasn't anything very witty. I just wanted to know if to give a French dictation you really had to be a French dictator. The trouble was, the friend laughed. Worse still, Mr. Palis heard him. His head snapped around so fast that his hearing aid nearly fell out. And somehow his eyes fell on me.

"Yes, Simple?" he said.

"I'm sorry, sir?" I asked with an innocent smile.

"Is there something I should know about? Something to give us all a good laugh?" By now he had strutted forward and my left ear was firmly wedged between his thumb and finger. "And what is the French for 'to laugh'?"

"I don't know, sir." I winced.

"It is *rire*. An irregular verb. *Je ris, tu ris, il rit* . . . I think you had better stay behind after school, Simple. And since you seem to like to laugh so much, you can write out for me the infinitive, participles, present indicative, past historic, future, and present subjunctive tenses of *rire*. Is that understood?"

"But, sir . . ."

"Are you arguing?"

"No, sir."

Nobody argued with Mr. Palis. Not unless you wanted to spend the rest of the day writing out the infinitive, participles, and all the restiples of the French verb *argumenter*.

So that was how I found myself on a sunny afternoon sitting in an empty classroom in an empty school struggling with the complexities of the last verb I felt like using. There was a clock ticking above the door. By four-fifteen I'd only gotten as far as the future. It looked as if my own future wasn't going to be that great. Then the door opened and Boyle and Snape walked in.

They were the last two people I'd expected to see. They were the last two people I *wanted* to see: Chief Inspector Snape of Scotland Yard and his very unlovely assistant Boyle. Snape was a great lump of a man who always looked as if he was going to burst out of his clothes, like the Incredible Hulk. He had pink skin and narrow eyes. Put a pig in a suit and you wouldn't be able to tell the difference until one of them went oink. Boyle was just like I remembered him: black hair— permed on his head, growing wild on his chest. Built like a boxer and I'm not sure if I mean the fighter or the dog. Boyle loved violence. And he hated me. I was only thirteen years old and he seemed to have made it his ambition to make sure that I wouldn't reach fourteen.

"Well, well, well," Snape muttered. "It seems we meet again."

"Pinch me," I said. "I must be dreaming."

Boyle's eyes lit up. "I'll pinch you!" He started toward me.

"Not now, Boyle!" Snape snapped.

"But he said—"

"It was a figure of speech."

Boyle scratched his head as he tried to figure it out. Snape sat on a desk and picked up an exercise book. "What's this?" he asked.

"It's French," I said.

"Yeah? Well, it's all Greek to me." He threw it aside and lit a cigarette. "So how are you keeping?" he asked.

"What are you doing here?" I replied. I had a feeling that they hadn't come to inquire about my health. The only inquiries those two ever made were the sort that people were helping them with.

"We came to see you," Snape said.

"Okay. Well, you've seen me now. So if you don't mind . . ." I reached for my book bag.

"Not so fast, laddie. Not so fast." Snape flicked ash into an inkwell. "The fact is, Boyle and me, we were wondering . . . we need your help."

"My help?"

Snape bit his lip. I could see he didn't like asking me. And

I could understand it. I was just a kid and he was a big shot in Scotland Yard. It hurt his professional pride. Boyle leaned against the wall and scowled. He would rather be hurting me.

"Have you heard of Johnny Powers?" Snape asked.

I shook my head. "Should I have?"

"He was in the papers last April. The front page. He'd just been sent down. He got fifteen years."

"That's too bad."

"Sure, especially as he was only fifteen years old." Snape blew out smoke. "The press called him Public Enemy Number One—and for once they were right. Johnny Powers started young . . ."

"How young?"

"He burned down his kindergarten. He committed his first armed robbery when he was eight years old. Got away with four crates of Mars bars and a barrel of Gatorade. By the time he was thirteen he was the leader of one of the most dangerous gangs in London. They were called the Slingshot Kids . . . which was quite a joke as they were using sawed-off shotguns. Johnny Powers was so crooked he even stole the saw."

There was a long silence.

"What's this got to do with me?" I asked.

"We got Powers last year," Snape went on. "Caught him red-handed trying to steal a million dollars' worth of designer clothes. When Johnny went shoplifting, you were lucky if you were left with the shop."

"So you've got him," I said. "What else do you want?"

"We want the man he was going to sell the clothes to."
Snape plunged his cigarette into the inkwell. There was a dull
hiss . . . but that might have been Boyle. "The Fence," he went
on. "The man who buys and distributes all the stolen prop-
erty in England . . . and in most of Europe, too.

"You see, Nick, crime is big business. Robberies, burglar-
ies, hijacks, heists . . . every year a mountain of stuff goes
missing. Silver candlesticks. Scotch whiskey. Japanese
stereos. You name it, somebody's stolen it. And recently we've
become aware that one man has set up an operation, a fan-
tastic network to handle it—buying and selling."

"You mean . . . like a shopkeeper?"

"That's just it. He could be a shopkeeper. He could be a
banker. He could be anyone. He doesn't get his hands dirty
himself, but he's got links with every gang this side of the
Atlantic. If we could get our hands on him, it would be a disaster for the underworld. And think of what he could tell us!
But he's an invisible man. We don't know what he looks like.
We don't know where he lives. To us he's just the Fence. And
we want him."

"We want him," Boyle repeated.

"I think I get the general idea, Boyle," I said. I turned
back to Snape. "So why don't you ask this Johnny Powers?"
I asked.

Snape lit another cigarette. "We have asked him," he
replied. "We offered to cut his sentence in half in return for
a name. But Powers is crazy. He refused."

"Honor among thieves," I muttered.

"Forget that," Snape said. "Powers would sell his own grandmother if it suited him. In fact he did sell her. She's now working in an Arabian salt mine. But he wouldn't sell her to a policeman. He hates policemen. He wouldn't tell us anything. On the other hand, he might just slip the name to someone he knew. Someone he was friendly with . . ."

"What are you getting at?" I asked. I was beginning to feel uneasy.

"Johnny Powers is fifteen," Snape went on. "Too young for prison—but too dangerous for reform school. So he was sent to a special maximum-security center just outside London—Strangeday Hall. It's for young offenders. No one there is over eighteen. But they're all hardened criminals. We want you to go there."

"Wait a minute . . . !" I swallowed. "I'm not a criminal. I'm not even hardened. I'm a softy. I like cuddly toys. I'm—"

"We'll give you a new name," Snape cut in. "A new identity. You'll share a cell with Powers. And as soon as you've found out what we want to know, we'll have you out of there. You'll be back at school before you even know it."

Out of one prison into another, I thought. But even if I could have skipped the whole term, I wouldn't have considered the offer. Snape might call Powers crazy, but that was the craziest thing I'd ever heard.

"Let me get this straight," I said. "You want to lock me up with some underage Al Capone in a maximum-security jail somewhere outside London. I'm to get friendly with him, preferably before I get my throat cut. And I'm to find out who this Fence is so you can arrest him, too."

"That's right." Snape smiled. "So what do you say?"

"Forget it! Absolutely not! You must be out of your mind, Snape! Not for a million bucks!"

"Can I take that as a no?" Snape asked.

I grabbed my bag and stood up. Mr. Palis and his irregular verbs could wait. I just wanted to get out of there. But at the same time Boyle lurched forward, blocking the way to the door. The look on his face could have blocked a drain.

"Let me persuade him, Chief," he said.

"No, Boyle . . ."

"But—"

"He's decided."

Snape swung himself off the desk. Boyle looked like he was going to explode, but he didn't try to stop me as I reached for the door handle.

"Give me a call if you change your mind," Snape muttered.

"Don't wait up for it," I said.

I left the two of them there and walked home. I didn't think I'd hear from them again. I mean, I'd told them what I thought of their crazy idea—and they could always find some other kid. The way I figured it was, they'd just forget about me and go and look for somebody else.

Which just shows you how much I knew.